Dreams of Magpie Cove

BOOKS BY KENNEDY KERR

MAGPIE COVE

The House at Magpie Cove

Secrets of Magpie Cove

Daughters of Magpie Cove

A Spell of Murder

Kennedy Kerr

Dreams of Magpie Cove

bookouture

Published by Bookouture in 2022

An imprint of Storyfire Ltd.
Carmelite House
50 Victoria Embankment
London EC4Y 0DZ

www.bookouture.com

ISBN: 978-1-80314-732-1
eBook ISBN: 978-1-80314-731-4

For the readers, with thanks

PROLOGUE

She sits on the edge of the bed, dressed in a hospital robe and tight surgical stockings. She is very aware that she is naked underneath the robe. It is as if all her authority as a grown-up has been taken away with her clothes, which are folded up neatly on a chair by the bed.

Don't worry. We'll make you look normal again after this, the surgeon assures her briskly in his well-spoken, no-nonsense voice.

What do you mean? she asks, wondering what he is going to do to her when she is asleep, other than what she knows he is going to do, which is horrific enough.

I mean, a reconstruction. We can rebuild the breast. Plastic surgery. He gives her a friendly nod, still brisk, which on one hand she appreciates – no point being coy or maudlin – but on the other, she resents, as if losing a breast was of no real concern at all.

Can I decide afterwards? she asks, and he nods.

Of course, of course, we can think about that later.

She wonders which medical school he went to. He is a little older than her, but not that much older. It's feasible they could have gone to the same university: he has that same well-bred assurance about him that so many of her university friends did. They came from money, and expected it to open doors as they grew up, qualified as doctors and lawyers and accountants, and strode confidently along a well-worn road of privilege.

She has managed to join their ranks, even though she doesn't come from money in the same way. Still, now, they accept her: *fake it until you make it,* isn't that the saying? She has faked it for years: keeping up with the clothes, the holidays, the skiing and the shooting weekends. All of it.

But all of her efforts matter little now, now that she is sitting on the edge of a hospital bed, a potentially deadly thing growing inside her, betraying her, the cells turning on themselves. What do designer clothes matter after you have received a possible death sentence?

She asks the surgeon, *Am I going to die?* She feels her gorge rise as she speaks the words, but she has to know, and she hasn't been brave enough to ask the question until now. Yet, it has been the only question in her mind since receiving the diagnosis. It's odd that he thinks she is worried about how she will *look* after the operation. All she is worried about is whether she will be alive in six months.

He reassures her that she is not going to die, not right now anyway, and that *survival rates are higher than ever before.*

Survival rates.

That is, there is a chance that she will not survive – either this surgery, or, more likely, the disease, in a matter of months or years. There is a calculation. There is a percentage chance applied to her survival, now.

She remembers that there was another relatively unlikely chance that she once mastered: an academic scholarship. At the time she had been told there was a ten per cent likelihood that she would be accepted to Oxford to study law, and, because she had worked for it, and because she was lucky perhaps, she had got it. She had conquered that ten per cent. And she had made it to the ranks of the blessed, fortunate ones and fought hard to stay there.

Surely, she has used up all her luck now? She isn't sure if she has the strength to fight to stay among the fortunate ones anymore. She lies down as instructed, and lets the kind nurses tuck the blankets around her as they prepare to wheel her bed down to the operating room.

We'll make you look normal again.

She repeats the phrase in her head as she watches the ceiling lights flash above her, being wheeled along the corridor. *Normal. What is normal?* she wonders as they open a door and wheel her into a kind of anteroom where the anaesthesiologist is waiting. *Can I ever be normal again after this? Do I want to be?*

She is told to count to ten, as the anaesthesiologist gently sticks something into the back of her hand. *I am counting away my life,* she thinks, just before she blacks out. *If I get through this, then I'm never going to waste another second. Whatever the odds. That's one thing I know.*

ONE

'Not bad for a drunken eBay purchase, Ellie McTavish.' Fiona rested one hand lightly on the black leather-covered steering wheel of the silver Airstream motorhome as they cruised along a deserted Cornish road, adjusting the ancient radio with the other. 'Will you see if *you* can get it to pick up an FM station. If it even does that.'

'Not sure if Cornwall has FM radio,' Ellie muttered, frowning as she twisted the radio dial. All she could find apart from static was some local news station talking about farming, or an oldies station somewhere which seemed to be playing a Dolly Parton medley. 'Or phone signal, come to that.'

'I know. Brilliant, isn't it? A proper break. Just what you need.' Fiona – though Ellie had only ever called her Fee in all the years they'd been friends – whistled happily to the faint strains of 'I Will Always Love You', returning both hands to the wheel.

'Maybe.' Ellie stared out of the window at the miles and miles of fields around them, populated with the occasional distant hamlet. Three or four houses at best, and that was it –

you'd passed through before you knew it; occasionally there was a pub or a post office-cum-corner shop.

And the further they drove into Cornwall, the stranger the place names got. Her favourites so far had been the village of Jolly Bottom and a hill tor signposted off the main road as Brown Willy. Fee's favourite was Compton Pauncefoot – a perfect name for a cat so she said – but that was much earlier in their drive down from London: around Somerset, in fact, which seemed like a world away, even though it was itself pretty far into the West Country.

In fact, Ellie had never been further south-west than Bristol before. She'd been born and raised in a featureless town in the middle of England, and gone to university in Oxford before heading to London in her early twenties to begin her high-flying legal career with one of the top firms there.

She hadn't had time for leisurely drives down to the seaside on the weekends: she was always working. And if she wasn't, there was always something: skiing with her colleagues at the law firm in France or Switzerland, weddings, expensive girls' weekends in Dubai or New York or Paris, parties at her friends' houses in Kensington or Holland Park, where the champagne flowed and if you didn't stay up drinking until the early hours you were considered some kind of social deviant. Not just that: you were expected to be in the office by seven in the morning the next day and finish at ten at night.

It wasn't that Ellie hadn't enjoyed that life, but she was ready to admit now, at the tender age of thirty-seven, that she was exhausted, and her body had finally said *no* to it all in a way that was difficult to ignore.

They'd stopped in a nice inn the night before and enjoyed a pretty pleasant meal in the pub, though Fee wouldn't let her have a glass of wine. *Not in your condition,* she'd admonished Ellie. *Healthy fruit juices only for you, my girl.* Ellie had protested: it wasn't like she was pregnant. But Fee was taking her job as Road Trip Manager and General Carer very seriously.

The shiny silver Airstream motorhome had attracted a fair bit of attention so far, she had to admit. At the inn – named The Fair Thee Well, somewhere in Devon – the manager had asked her about it, but she hadn't felt like talking much, leaving it to Fee to explain that they had decided on a road trip down to Cornwall for a while, though she'd avoided explaining why. They'd agreed that Ellie could tell people if she wanted to, but otherwise Fee wouldn't mention it.

Since she'd found the lump in her breast, she'd spent every night staring up at the dark ceiling of her flat, with the worst-case scenarios running through her mind.

I might have only months to live.

I'll die in terrible pain.

I'm only thirty-seven. There's still so much I want to do.

It's so unfair. Why me? Why now? What's wrong with me? What did I do to cause all this?

It had only taken a few weeks from diagnosis to surgery: apparently, her cancer was reasonably aggressive, and her doctor wasn't taking any chances that it wouldn't grow any more than it had. When he'd operated, it was the size of a tangerine.

She was grateful that it had been taken care of so fast. She knew that was what you were supposed to say, and what you were supposed to think. When people asked her about it, when she had to talk to the HR officer at her firm on the phone, she'd said all the things you were supposed to say to make other people feel better about cancer.

They found it really early.

The doctors were marvellous.

Everything happened really quickly.

I'm staying positive.

Three of those four statements were true.

The breast was taken away, and she'd been sent home with

instructions on how to look after the wound, as well as some pretty heavy-duty painkillers and a course of a hormonal therapy drug intended to stop any new cancer growing.

However, she didn't feel positive. In fact, after the surgery, Ellie felt numb inside. She knew that the surgery had had to be done, and she understood that the doctors were acting in her best interest. But it was all so sudden.

It was only now, that she'd had it, that she realised how much of the experience of cancer was looking after other people's feelings. Ellie didn't have many people close to her, but even the incidental people in her life wanted the reassurance. The postman. The lady that delivered her supermarket order. The community nurse that came to change her dressings and check how she was doing. All of them wanted to hear how positive she felt, so she told them. She plastered on a smile and assuaged their worry, because she understood that what they were really saying was, *Tell me it's okay, because I'm afraid that I'll get this, and I want to know it's going to be okay if I do. That it's not a big deal.*

She gave them what they wanted. She made out that she was the hotshot professional woman that was so positive and fit and successful that she'd be back in the office in a week in a new Versace outfit and that you could totally get the better of cancer. It was all just Positive Mental Attitude.

And every time she did it, it made Ellie more tired. It took something away from her.

Ellie wasn't great at processing her emotions at the best of times. Emotions, she had realised, over the years, were best ignored. She was a lawyer. She was good at concentrating on the facts.

She'd decided long ago to create a life where she had to feel as little as humanly possible, and she'd pretty much succeeded. Ellie was single and had one close friend. Her mum had died when she was at university, and her parents were divorced: her dad had moved to Spain with his new wife when she was ten. She had no children and that was all totally fine with her.

But now, she found herself at home, alone, in her flat, recuperating from surgery with nothing to do but feel things, and she didn't like it.

Being a lawyer had provided her with a daily life of the gym, power lunches and long hours in the office or in court, coupled with nights drinking expensive wine in posh bars. And if she wasn't doing that, she was at the beauty salon or the hairdresser having a facial or her nails done or having her long black wavy hair blow-dried straight. She had to look the part in court and in the office. She had to be perfect at all times.

Being perfect was a great distraction from enduring your feelings, Ellie was discovering. She flicked the channels from one retired couple looking for a house in Spain to an American soap that had been on when she was at Oxford, almost twenty years ago, to a daytime chat show where the hosts were discussing the best healthy breakfasts.

She kept crying, on and off. It was like a tap she couldn't turn off. Some of it was tiredness, and a kind of release of the worry she'd been building up before the operation. She didn't have a Positive Mental Attitude. In fact, she was in a state of grief.

Nothing like this had ever happened to Ellie before. Yes, she'd had to work hard to get a scholarship to Oxford, and she'd worked hard in her career, but that was a challenge she'd enjoyed. That wasn't like this. This was... she didn't have words for it. It was like being punched. Like someone had broken into her flat and trashed it. It was as alien an experience as anything she could think of.

There was normal life, running along happily in its groove, and then there was being told you had cancer, which was like falling into a sudden earthquake. All the usual rules suddenly did not apply. Ellie felt that she had been abruptly removed from normal life by some kind of Martian overlord and plonked down in a world she didn't recognise at all. A world of tests and anxiety and the smell of antiseptic and the beeping of machines. Of sudden surgery, without being given the time to prepare her feelings.

And now, here she was, a few weeks later, in bed, watching *Cash in the Attic* and feeling like she couldn't stop crying.

Plus, she'd bid on the motorhome late one night, in the days after she'd had the mastectomy, and now she had no idea what to do with it.

Ellie still wasn't quite sure what had possessed her to do it, but it might have had something to do with the two glasses of wine she'd drunk as she lay on the sofa, watching a depressing movie about a mother who had lost her child. She wasn't supposed to be drinking at all, what with the painkillers she was on, but she'd been desperate to numb her brain, which kept whirring around and around, imagining the worst. *What if the cancer comes back? What about all the things I haven't done? Why aren't I married?*

She'd been depressed and terrified and desperate for any distraction. She couldn't sleep, because she was uncomfortable, despite the painkillers, and she still had a tube taped to her chest which was draining liquid into a plastic bulb. Apparently, this was standard procedure, and the drain was supposed to stay in for about two weeks. It was towards the end of week two already, and the drain was a monumental pain in the behind. Ellie had realised that the tube got caught up in her clothes really easily and had to be taped to her side to make sure it didn't accidentally get ripped out. She couldn't wear anything that had to be taken off over her head because it was hard to move her arm on her left side, and the drain tubes got in the way.

The night she'd bought the motorhome, she'd opened her laptop, her fingers hovering over her work email icon. She was actually signed off for six weeks, and HR had told her to check in after five; she could let them know if she wanted to be off for longer. They'd been very good about everything, but Ellie knew that although her assistant was supposed to be looking at her inbox for her, and though she'd handed over her main clients to a colleague, her emails were still going to get out of hand really quickly.

Still, she resisted the urge to look at her emails, and tapped the eBay icon instead.

Ellie's friend Toni had introduced Ellie to eBay in her first term in halls, and initially Ellie had welcomed a bargain website where she could find a new top for £5 or less, or some winter boots that she needed. But Toni and some of the others on the law course had made a game of it, buying the most random items they could at the last minute. They'd called it the Last-Minute Bid for Glory.

Ellie's new friends thought nothing of spending hundreds of pounds on stupid things they didn't need, all for a laugh. Ellie was on an academic scholarship, and accounted for every penny she spent. She had all the loans she could get on top of that, and even then she was only just making ends meet. By contrast, Toni and the rest of them threw money around as if it was confetti at a wedding.

Once, Toni had bought a goat on eBay. A real, live goat. It had been delivered to her halls by a guy in a van, and she'd got a serious telling-off from the warden, who had ended up taking it home to live in his sister's garden. Goodness only knew why anyone was selling a goat on a general auction website: it was clearly dodgy.

Another time, one of their friends, Giles, had bought a car and then given it away to some guy in the local pub because there was nowhere to park it on campus. Last-minute purchases were always accompanied by much celebration and drunken whooping. It had always seemed amusing at the time, though

Ellie marvelled that no one's parents ever seemed to mind that their children were spending hundreds of pounds on nothing in particular in late-night drunken splurges. At least, none of her friends ever talked about it if they did.

A couple of months before Ellie had been due to leave for Oxford, her mum had been diagnosed with cancer. She'd shooed Ellie away, even though Ellie had wanted to defer a year and stay at home to be there for her. But her mum wouldn't hear of it. She had been so proud of Ellie: the first person in their family to go to university.

Make me proud, she'd said as she hugged Ellie at the train station. *I know you will. And I'm already so proud of you, my lovely girl.*

Ellie had watched her university friends throwing their money around and, every time, she thought about her mum who couldn't work now, because she was ill, living on benefits and refusing to let Ellie drop out of university to get a job to help her. She thought about her mum's house, which didn't have central heating, and how her mum wrapped herself up in so many blankets at night to keep warm that they joked she looked like the Michelin Man.

She thought about how the money for just one of those stupid online purchases could have paid her mum's winter electricity bill, or bought her a whole month's worth of food and still provided change for her weekly bus ride to the hospital. But she never said anything to her friends, because what could she say? They wouldn't understand.

When her mum had passed away two years later, Ellie hadn't wanted to tell any of them. Toni had found out because she'd walked into Ellie's room one night and found her crying. In fact, once they knew, her friends had been incredibly kind. They had asked Ellie to come and stay with their families, taken her on holiday, made her their plus one at dinners and events and all the stuff she could never have afforded to do otherwise.

They weren't bad people: they had just never known what it was to be poor, or cold, or hungry.

In a way, it was losing Ellie's mum that had made her a part of that moneyed, affluent gang. They had taken care of her at her lowest ebb, and she felt a loyalty to them.

Ellie had played Last-Minute Bid for Glory, but she had never bought anything expensive because she couldn't afford it. But that evening in her flat, recovering from a mastectomy, tipsy, tearful and feeling like she just didn't care about anything anymore, she had opened up the online auction site and refreshed the home page.

And there, just about to close, was a 1985 Airstream motorhome, complete with original awnings, a working ice maker, oven and gas stove, and twin beds. She'd entered a stupid bid, closed her eyes, and passed out on the sofa.

In the morning, she'd found the email confirming that she'd bought the damn thing.

TWO

'St Ives should be about ten miles up this road.' Ellie peered at her map and then at an outcrop of small white signposts half-hidden in a tall hawthorn hedge. 'Yeah. I think it's pointing that way. Look.'

'Bloody hope so. The roads have been getting narrower and narrower since we left that A road. Marilyn was made for wide highways, not these bloody tiny lanes,' Fee grumbled, putting the motorhome back into Drive and setting off again. 'Can't say I'm getting used to the left-hand drive yet either.' Fee had nick-named the motorhome Marilyn, and the name suited its faded silvery glamour and rounded curves.

'I could drive. She is mine, you know,' Ellie offered, knowing that Fee wouldn't let her behind the wheel. Her chest was healing, but she did feel weak still, and sitting up for long periods of time was tiring. The good thing about the motorhome was that it had beds, and Ellie could go and lie down whenever she wanted. Inside, most of the features were still original, down to the gas hob, the cleverly designed cupboards and the fold-out table that they'd sat at earlier, stopping en route from the Devon inn when they found an amazing view over Dartmoor.

'Don't be daft. You can pass me some fudge, though.'

Ellie dutifully reached into the box on the long dashboard in front of her and passed Fee a silver-wrapped piece of fudge they'd picked up yesterday at a garage.

It was strange, not having the routine of her ordinary life to structure her days. Gone were the days of being up at five thirty to go for a run from her flat overlooking the river in Vauxhall, across the bridge and along the Embankment and into the City, to get to work by six thirty in time for a shower, do her hair and make-up and get dressed, to be at her desk around seven.

She had a full-length locker in the capacious changing rooms of the gym, which she went to three times a week, and kept a rotation of work outfits in it, pressed and ready. She kept at least two pairs of heels in her office, though if she wasn't needed in any meetings that day – a rare occurrence – she'd go barefoot or wear slippers under her desk. Her firm had once had a policy that all female employees were required to wear high heels, and although that had now been firmly outlawed, Ellie felt that there was still an expectation.

For the past few weeks, though, she'd slept in late, and eaten whatever she wanted. Not that she wanted much, at first, after the operation, but gradually her appetite was starting to come back. She'd been on a vegan macrobiotic diet for years – not including the booze, which was seen as a kind of necessary evil by her friends – to keep her figure at a size 8, which, at thirty-seven, was a lot harder than it had been when she was twenty-five.

Ellie would never usually have eaten fudge – pure cream and sugar! – but she didn't feel like she cared anymore. And, as Fee – who had never dieted in her life – had pointed out, Ellie would have a hard time eating as a macrobiotic vegan in Cornwall, the land of pasties, cream teas and fish and chips. Last night at the inn, they'd had steak pie, chips and gravy, followed by banoffee pie, and it had been glorious.

Ellie's operation had been three weeks ago, and by now she could walk around and function reasonably well. Her drain had been taken out by an efficient, friendly district nurse the week before, and she had daily exercises to do. She was still on the painkillers, but at a lower dosage. She still had a large dressing on her scar which she changed daily: the nurse had given her a supply of everything to take with her.

Fee had suggested they had two weeks away, touring Devon and Cornwall in Marilyn, since Ellie had been crazy enough to buy her. Fee was a freelance graphic designer, so she could work from the road if she needed to, but she'd set aside the time to be pretty much available for Ellie. *I haven't taken any time off this year, anyway*, she'd said when she'd visited Ellie the week before. *Come on. Why don't we take her for a road trip?*

Ellie had decided not to think about work for now. She needed to get away from London, not least because her boss had already dropped in with a lavish fruit basket and casually asked her if she thought she'd be back before six weeks.

Ellie knew if she stayed in her flat, she'd start looking at her emails, and from there, it was just a hop, skip and a jump to being back at her desk, insisting that she was fine, and plunging back into a work culture that didn't allow for part-time work. Too often she'd seen female colleagues coming back to work after their maternity leave edged out of their jobs by expectations that the long hours and the after-work drinks and meals out weren't optional. Requests for flexible working were usually rejected, as were shortened weeks or even job shares after female employees had babies. If you had kids and had to leave work for a childcare emergency, or just had to leave at a certain time to pick up your kid from nursery, faces were pulled and you were seen as 'dropping the ball' or 'not being a team player'. You had to be seen to be doing the hours, at the drinks and hobnobbing with the powers-that-be, no matter how good your work was.

Ellie had seen it all, and she knew that some people probably already thought that getting cancer was a sign of weakness on her part. Or that perhaps she wasn't as committed to her health as she could be. Even Toni had, after enquiring whether she was going skiing the next month to their usual exclusive French resort (clearly, she wasn't), had told her how wonderful wheatgrass had been in helping clear up her skin. *It's some kind of wonder drug, especially with ginger in a smoothie,* she'd said, her eyes darting to Ellie's loose button-through top, under which some of her chest bandage could be seen. *I've heard that it can actually cure cancer.*

That had really hurt. Ellie knew Toni and Suzanne thought they were being helpful, but Ellie had wanted to scream at them, *Do you think wheatgrass will bring back the feeling under my arm? How much ginger do I have to consume to stop waking up in the night because I can still feel my phantom breast and it hurts? And please tell me how this wonder drink could have saved my mum's life. If only us poor people had known about wheatgrass then! How our lives would be different.*

'You know, you were the only friend that came to see me that actually asked me how I was.' Ellie looked at her friend as they drove along. 'Not many people came to see me at all. My boss just wanted to know when I was coming back, and Toni and Suzanne spent all fifteen minutes of their visit trying to tell me that if I'd only stuffed a rose quartz egg up my fanny, none of this would ever have happened.'

Fee snorted. 'Did they really? Idiots. I've said it before, Ellie. I really don't know why you hang out with those guys.'

'They're my friends,' Ellie protested. Despite the fact that Toni and Suzanne had really hurt her feelings, Toni had been the one that had made her come and stay at her parents' holiday home in Kos after Ellie's mum's funeral. They'd spent the whole summer together on the beach with some of the others from their course, all staying at Toni's parents' large villa, swimming, drinking and taking boat tours around the islands.

'Are they?' Fee raised an eyebrow.

'You know what I mean. We're a group. It's a work thing.'

'If they don't care about you when you had breast cancer, Ellie, they're not your friends.'

Ellie wondered what had changed. She couldn't have asked for better friends after her mum died, but now, it felt like she was being ignored. Everyone was getting older, of course; some of her friends had young families now, and because she didn't, they naturally had less in common. But it wasn't just that. Something had shifted, imperceptibly, and she didn't know what it was.

Perhaps it was her. Perhaps she had changed.

'Hmm. Lucky I've got you, then.' Ellie fluttered her eyelashes at Fee. Fee had been Ellie's first flatmate when she'd moved to London, back in the days when she'd got her first law job. They'd been so young, then: Fee had a job as a junior graphic designer at a fancy firm in the West End that treated her terribly, and Ellie routinely worked late into the night.

They were both busy, but on the nights when they got home at a decent hour, they'd pour themselves a large gin and tonic each or share a bottle of wine and watch the weekly soaps, laughing at the terrible storylines and over-the-top acting. Sometimes they'd go along to each other's work drinks, or go dancing. Eventually, Ellie had moved out to live on her own when she could afford it, but they'd stayed friends.

'You are blessed—'

Fee broke off, frowning, and tapped the control panel in front of the steering wheel. At the same time, there was a crunching sound, and Fee swore and stood on the brakes. They came to a stop, fortunately with no other cars around them, in the middle of the narrow road.

'What happened?' Ellie leaned over and looked at the

speedometer. A couple of red lights had flickered on. 'What does that mean?'

Fee pulled on the handbrake and turned the key in the ignition a few times, off and on. Nothing happened.

'I think we've broken down,' she said, trying the ignition again. Nothing happened. 'Ugh! This is a nightmare!'

'I suppose this is what you get for buying a vintage motorhome.' Ellie groaned.

'Do you have the guy's number? The guy you bought it from?' Fee asked. 'Maybe he can help. Did he tell you that it had anything wrong with it?'

'Of course not.' Ellie rolled her eyes. 'And before you ask, no, I didn't ask. I was a bit out of it at the time.' She sighed. 'I think it would be better to call a recovery truck and go from there. See if we can get towed to a local garage. Hopefully it's nothing too tricky to fix and we can be on our way again.'

'Okay. I think I've got a signal.' Fee peered at her phone, and tapped at the screen for a few moments. 'Right. Here's a garage with a tow service that says it's, like, five miles away. I'll give them a call.' She stepped out of the cab and walked up the narrow road, which was bordered on both sides with tall hedges. This seemed to be a characteristic of Cornwall. Only occasionally would the hedges thin or disappear altogether, and Ellie was able to see across lush green fields or into deep forests.

Earlier in the morning, they had driven down a road through a sparse village that ended with perhaps a mile of a stream bordering the road and filled with unusually mossy trees with long, serpentine branches that seemed to flow back into the black earth underneath them. Fee had commented that there was a very strange feeling there as they drove along that road: not a bad feeling, but more like it was enchanted somehow. That this was a different kind of place, an old place with old tree spirits. *You can imagine witches and fairies here*, she'd mused as they drove Marilyn along slowly.

It was certainly different to London, and Ellie didn't mind that at all. She was happy to be far away from everything and everyone, and even happier not to have a reliable phone signal.

Fee returned to the cab and pulled herself up into the driver's seat.

'Okay. Spoke to a guy and he's going to come and tow us to his garage. He's somewhere called Magpie Cove. Sounds quaint, doesn't it? We'll either find somewhere to stay, or we can sleep in Marilyn. All right?'

'All right.' Ellie smiled at her friend. 'We're having an adventure,' she added, firmly.

'We are indeed.' Fee shook her head, grinning.

THREE

Though they'd sat in the front of the pickup truck with the mechanic all the way to Magpie Cove – his name was Mark, he said, confirmed on the side of his truck as Mark Gardner Repairs – Ellie and Fee didn't learn much about him other than the fact that he'd lived in the tiny coastal village of Magpie Cove all his life.

It wasn't for lack of trying, mostly on Fee's part: even just five miles' drive along the twisty road, carefully towing Marilyn's sashaying curves behind them, seemed to take forever with someone who either gave one-word answers or grunted in response to questions. Eventually, Fee gave up and exchanged a glance with Ellie, who had to hide her smile by staring out of the window. Mark Gardner was definitely the strong and silent type.

He was also pretty easy on the eye, although Ellie would never have mentioned it to Fee. She had always been shy about that kind of thing, and she'd rarely allowed herself the time for romantic relationships. There had been some over the years, but nothing that had lasted very long. Either her work got in the way, or, if she started seeing someone within her social group, there was always too much peer pressure.

The two times she'd gone out with someone from the 'fortunate ones', as Fee called them, the other women in the group seemed to want to marry them off to each other so that they had another lavish wedding to look forward to. Or, there was jealousy from somewhere else in the group. It was all too much of a pressure cooker for Ellie, who disliked all the in-fighting and gossip that came from being part of a group that spent almost all of its time socialising and working together.

Still, there was no denying that this guy was good-looking. Ellie assumed he was likely very popular with the local women – or men, perhaps. He wore dark blue overalls with his name stitched over the pocket and a company logo on the back, and some heavy work boots. However, he obviously either worked out or maybe car repairs were more strenuous than she thought, because his rolled-up sleeves revealed tanned, muscular forearms, and – if you were looking, which Ellie most definitely wasn't – his shoulders and biceps strained at the rough blue material.

He didn't have a perfect face – who did, in real life? Ellie knew from experience that most people who did had paid a lot of money to achieve that kind of bland perfection. But though the lines on his forehead and around his eyes meant he wasn't twenty anymore, he had handsome features, with blue eyes that regarded you with an earnest, slightly guarded expression, and blond hair that curled onto his collar.

Mark drove the truck down a winding lane, and Ellie glimpsed a sudden flash of blue between a row of cottages.

'Oh! We're by the sea?' she cried out, surprised.

Mark caught her eye and a sudden, warm smile broke out on his serious face. 'Magpie Cove. Used to be a fishing village – well, still is, a bit, but not 'ow it was. We gets surfers down 'ere in the summer. Still quiet most days, though, 'specially at dawn.

T'other mornin', I had a whole purple-red sunrise to myself, out on the cove.'

'Wow. I don't think I've ever seen the sun rise over the sea.' Ellie looked back at Mark, whose cheeks had blushed as red as the sun he described. She wasn't sure why – was he that shy? 'I used to run along the Thames most mornings, from my flat to the office. Quite often I'd catch the sunrise then. It's a really great feeling, isn't it?'

'Can't beat it,' he mumbled, looking back at the road.

They pulled into a wide courtyard bordered with a varnished wooden fence and a sign outside that said: 'Mark Gardner Repairs: Autos, Haulage and Vintage'.

Fee hopped out of her side of the cab and helped Ellie out of hers. Mark watched Ellie take her time getting down the wide steps, but said nothing.

He walked into a Portacabin labelled 'Office' and came back with some forms on a clipboard, thrusting them awkwardly at Fee.

'So. I'll have a poke round in the motorhome. Not likely to get 'er started again today, though, so you'll need to stay somewhere local, or I can let you stay 'ere overnight if you want. There's a café in the village you can get your dinner at.'

'Are there many places to stay in Magpie Cove? B&Bs, that kind of thing?' Fee gave Ellie a concerned glance. 'I mean, we're supposed to be on a road trip. We don't mind staying a night or two, but...'

'Esther Christie takes in guests sometimes.' He shrugged. 'Dunno otherwise. I can give Esther a call if you want? She's got a cottage down the harbour. She'll see you right.'

'Well, why don't we stay in Marilyn tonight and see where we are tomorrow?' Ellie suggested. She felt very tired, all of a sudden, and the thought of trudging off into the village to a B&B felt like being asked to climb Everest. 'Is that okay, Mark?

You can trust us. We'll just stay inside. She's got everything we need.'

'Fine with me,' he said, handing Fee a pen. 'I just need your details on the form, and I'll get right on it. Fair warnin', your motorhome's a foreign vintage model, so if she needs parts, that might get expensive, and none too quick, either. I got a couple of vintage parts dealers I use, but it's not like gettin' a new gearbox for a Ford. All right?'

'Actually, it's Ellie's motorhome, not mine.' Fee handed the paperwork to Ellie. 'But, okay, we understand.'

'Do you think it's something big? Or an easy repair?' Ellie took the clipboard and scanned it. Most of the information it was asking for she had no idea about. There was some ownership paperwork stashed in the glove box; she'd hardly looked at it when Betsy and Colin, the sellers, a couple in their late sixties, had dropped Marilyn off in the gated parking area of her exclusive apartment complex. As much as anything, Ellie had agreed to Fee's road-trip idea so that she could get Marilyn out from under the baleful gaze of the building manager, who seemed to want to tell her every day that her apartment came with one allocated parking space only, and Marilyn was taking up four.

'Hard to say. Could be anythin'.' Mark looked at Ellie with some curiosity. 'You 'ad 'er long?'

'What, me? No. A week and a half.'

'You into vintage cars 'n' that?' He frowned at Ellie and then at Marilyn.

Ellie thought that he was probably wondering why on earth she'd bought a 1980s American motorhome, but she wasn't about to explain the whole cancer-and-eBay fiasco now. 'No. It was... an impulse purchase,' she explained lamely. Mark raised his eyebrows, but said nothing. 'Fee, I need to lie down, okay?'

She turned away from where the three of them were standing and walked as composedly as she could over to Marilyn, which had now been taken off the haulage truck and was sitting normally on all four wheels. She got herself up the three wide steps into Marilyn's warm, comfy interior and headed for the bedroom at the back. Fee had been sleeping on the pull-out sofa.

'Ellie? Are you okay? Ellie?' Fee had followed her, but Ellie was suddenly too exhausted to reply.

'I just need to sleep,' she muttered, as she sank onto the covers and half pulled one of them over her legs. Her chest wound hurt, though it had been healing nicely, and she felt like she could sleep for weeks.

FOUR

'Ellie. Hey, Ellie. Wake up.' Fee's voice woke her, and Ellie opened her eyes blearily.

'What happened?' she whispered, blinking in the light. Fee had opened the blue and red tartan curtains in the bedroom part of the motorhome. Marilyn's whole décor wasn't exactly Ellie's style, but she hadn't been overly bothered about changing anything in it. She planned to sell it after the road trip.

'You passed out when we got here, remember? Here, I walked into the village and got us some bacon rolls and coffee. There's a great little bakery down there. Maude's Fine Buns, it's called. And there's a really nice café, too, so we won't starve. It's just a few streets away.'

Fee placed a paper bag next to Ellie on the bed, and set a takeaway cup of coffee on the small table that was bolted to the floor next to it.

'Thanks.' Ellie sat up groggily, reached for the coffee and sipped it. 'Oh. This is good. I expected instant.'

'I guess you can still get good coffee down here in the middle of nowhere.' Fee grinned. 'Don't let your bacon roll get cold,' she added, as she bit into hers. 'Mark's working on the engine as we speak. He started on it yesterday but he hasn't said much yet. I don't think he says much as a rule, actually.'

'The strong, silent type.' Ellie yawned. 'I didn't know they actually existed.'

'That's because all the guys you know are lawyers.' Fee sipped her coffee. 'If I was into guys, though, I would definitely ask him for a tune-up. He's like the Brad Pitt of Cornwall.'

'I hadn't noticed,' Ellie lied.

Fee snorted. 'Come on. You might be convalescing but you're not dead.' She looked mortified as soon as she'd said it. 'Ellie, I'm so sorry, I didn't mean—'

'What? I'm *not* dead. Very happy to be alive, in fact.' Ellie took a bite of the bacon roll, and almost gasped. The bacon was thick, salty and perfectly cooked, and the bun was the softest brioche roll she thought she'd ever had. 'My God, this is amazing.' She chewed for a second and started to feel more human. 'I'm so sorry. Were you okay here last night? I think the painkillers knocked me out a bit, and the travelling. I didn't realise I was still so tired.'

'You're going to take a while to recover, Ellie. You just haven't actually listened to your body for years. You can't thrash it like a sports car anymore and expect it to be okay.'

'I guess so.' Ellie drank more coffee. 'Pass me my pills, would you?' She looked at the packets. She had plenty of the anti-cancer drug that the doctor had started her on, but the painkillers were coming to an end. It was true – she knew she didn't need them as much anymore, but she still felt a sense of slight panic realising that she was running out of *the hard stuff*, as Fee called it.

'Want to come down to the beach? I saw it from the high street. It looks beautiful,' Fee asked, tactfully changing the subject. 'It's not far. We can sit down when we get there, I saw benches.'

'Okay. Let me have a shower and get up first, though.'

Marilyn had a surprisingly capacious bathroom, and there was a water tank incorporated in the motorhome that only needed topping up every few days, which was easy to do if you called into a campsite.

Ellie caught sight of her reflection in the mirror at the other side of the room and made a face. 'I look awful.'

'You look disgustingly gorgeous, just like you always do.' Fee swatted Ellie playfully on the arm and stood up, screwing up the paper bag her roll had come in. 'I'll see you outside.'

In the shower, Ellie found it hard to look at her scar. She was so used to her breasts just being there, it was weird now that one of them was gone. It felt wrong. Unbalanced. And it looked horrible to Ellie, even though the surgeon had been as neat as he could.

He'd assured her that not only could she have reconstructive surgery, but that the scars would heal and fade, and eventually no one would ever know that she'd had a mastectomy at all. *Don't worry. We'll make you look normal again* – wasn't that what he'd said?

Normal.

Whatever that was.

The thing was that she didn't know if she really felt up to reconstruction surgery. She didn't know if she really wanted one fake boob. It felt... weird. In normal circumstances, she'd never have chosen plastic surgery, so why do it now?

Because you look like a freak. That's why, her inner voice muttered as she towelled herself dry. *In the event that a man is ever interested in you, then he's going to run screaming once he sees that. Run from the Terrifying One-Breasted Woman.*

She was used to that voice. It was relentless. It was the same voice that told her she was fat, that she needed to work out more, that she absolutely shouldn't get a Chinese takeaway after a long work week because it was full of calories and salt, and that she'd never be as pretty or as successful as the other women she worked with.

That voice had kept her on a diet since she was twenty. Seventeen years of self-denial.

Tears welled up in Ellie's eyes. It was a cruel thing to say to anyone, never mind yourself.

I'm not a freak, she argued back. *I'm me. And I didn't choose this. Maybe I don't want a reconstruction. Maybe, if someone likes me, then they'll like me for who I am, however many boobs I have. If you love someone, then none of that matters.*

Yeah, right, said the voice. *Keep telling yourself that, and see where it gets you.*

Fee knocked on the door. 'Hey. You okay in there? Mark's here. He's got an update about Marilyn.'

'I'll be right out,' Ellie called, clutching the towel around her, even though Fee couldn't see her. She looked at herself in the mirror again, and looked away quickly. *I'm ugly,* she thought, her heart sinking. *Why did this happen? Why did it happen to me? I hate this. I hate my body. I hate myself.*

She reached for the soft cotton bralette the doctors had recommended she wear as her scar healed. For now, she had to go lopsided; for when the scar was up to it, the nurse had given her a prosthetic breast she could put in the missing side. She shuddered at the thought of it.

She remembered when she'd got her first bra, and her mum had made her wear it to school. She hadn't wanted to. It was embarrassing. It made her feel different. She felt like everyone was looking at her. This was exactly the same. The only improvement was that Tom Johnson and his gang weren't sneaking up to her in the middle of science and snapping her bra strap for laughs.

On the other hand, she'd just had cancer. Compared to

cancer, Tom Johnson and the bra-snapping lads in the science lab were a walk in the park.

Being between a size 8 and a 10 and having been a workout addict and constant dieter for seventeen years, she only wore an A cup. Maybe she would have felt more conspicuous now, after the mastectomy, if she'd had Fee's more voluptuous figure – the loss would have been more noticeable, perhaps. But even if she wore one of the many loose blouses she'd bought online for the road trip, and even with her petite figure, she still felt like people were looking at her. That they knew what had happened to her, and that they knew what her body looked like.

That she looked like a freak.

Ellie reached for her knickers, pulled on her jeans and buttoned up the white blouse, turning up the sleeves. She tied her wavy black hair up in a ponytail and put on some basic make-up. Nothing fancy, but she was suddenly tired of seeing herself in the mirror so washed out. *Fake it till you make it*, she grinned at herself aggressively in the mirror. She looked like a crazy woman. Still, to someone who didn't know her, she looked slightly more normal than before.

That was probably as good as she was going to get right now.

FIVE

'Sorry to be the bearer of bad news.' Mark wiped his hands on a rag. 'If you want ter get 'er back on the road, it's gonna to take a whole new transmission, and I won't be able ter get 'old of one for a few weeks at least. As I said, vintage American parts aren't easy to come by.'

'A few weeks?' Ellie looked at him, unable to process what he was saying. 'But I've got to be back in London by then, more or less. We're supposed to be on a road trip!'

Mark shrugged apologetically. 'Sorry. I'm amazed you made it this far, to be honest. Take it you didn't 'ave a mechanic look at it before you bought it?'

Ellie hadn't, but she didn't want to explain why. She shook her head, hating the fact that he probably thought she was some stupid woman that didn't know anything about cars. She didn't, in fact, but normally she would never have bought a second-hand motorhome with an almost dead transmission – whatever that was. How to explain that she'd been in a desolate painkiller-and-surgery-induced fugue when she'd bought it?

'No, I didn't,' she said, curtly. 'How much will it cost to fix?'

Mark gave her the number, which made her flinch.

'I mean, she's vintage, so if she were restored and repaired, she'd 'ave decent resale value,' he explained. 'People love these Airstreams now. I restored a motorhome last year for a woman, she wanted to use it as a food truck. What I'm saying is, I'm 'appy to do it. But it's gonna take time and money, and you might not wanna do it.'

'I can afford it,' Ellie retorted. 'It's not that. It's the time.' She turned to Fee. 'You had a whole route worked out. We didn't plan to be stuck in the back of beyond.'

She knew it was a rude remark as soon as she'd said it, and Mark's face showed that he thought so too. She wanted to take it back, but the moment had gone, and anyway, she hardly knew the man.

Fee frowned. 'Well, it is pretty nice here. Why don't we go down to the beach and have a think about it? Mark, can we let you know when we get back? We'll just be an hour or so.'

''Course.' He shaded his eyes from the sun. 'I'll be 'ere. As I said, Esther Christie sometimes takes in guests at her cottage. It's down near the cove.' He gave them the address on a piece of paper. 'If you're going into the village, give 'er a knock and ask.'

'Okay. Thanks. We'll see you soon.' Fee took Ellie's arm and steered her towards the garage gateway. 'Be nice,' she muttered, under her breath, so that only Ellie could hear. 'This guy's helping us out, you know. He didn't have to let us stay here last night. He could have turfed us out of Marilyn, but he knew you were spark out in the back.'

Ellie sighed. 'I know, I know.'

They walked up the road and left onto a narrow lane which led out onto a small high street. As Fee had described, there was a welcoming-looking café in the middle with a small bakery opposite and a sign above another building that proclaimed it as a Shipwreck and Smuggling Museum. Along the street a little, they passed a butcher's shop and an antiques shop with a 'Closed' sign in the window. There was also a small art gallery, a couple of houses and what looked like a catering business at the end of the street.

'Pretty, isn't it?' Fee asked. 'Cobbled streets! Independent businesses! I like it.'

'It's okay,' Ellie agreed, reluctantly. She was more of a city girl at heart, though she could see that Magpie Cove was very quaint. *Chocolate box appeal*, she thought, remembering a phrase from one of the daytime property shows she'd been watching since she'd been at home. Wasn't that what it was called?

'Well, I like it.' Fee took Ellie's arm. 'And... ta dah! Not bad, eh?'

A horseshoe-shaped yellow sandy cove opened up before them, with the sun sparkling on the sapphire-blue water. Ellie had to admit that it was breath-taking. Craggy cliffs rose around the cove to the right, and a rocky escarpment led out into the water on the left. Ellie could just see beyond it into another cove where a few houses dotted the shore. In the cove in front of her, one beach house sat to the right where the sandy cove met the mainland.

Ellie stared out at the brilliant blue sea. A group of people were bobbing around, midway out towards the horizon. 'Okay. Yes, it's really nice.' Ellie gave Fee a grudging smile. 'But I can't see us staying here for weeks, can you?'

'Well, let's find this Esther what's-her-name.' Fee waved the piece of paper Mark had given her under Ellie's nose. 'She might have some kind of amazing place that might change your mind.'

They followed Mark's directions and found the cottage. Ellie knocked on the door, and then again, louder, when no one answered. A man's head with a bushy white beard appeared out of the window above.

'Can I 'elp you?' he shouted down.

'Is Esther here? Mark Gardner told us to come and see her about bed and breakfast,' Ellie shouted up to him.

'Naw. She's down at the beach, 'avin a swim. Be back dreckly,' the man answered in a broad Cornish accent. 'If I were thee, I'd go an' find 'er at the cove.'

'Right. Okay, we will,' Fee replied, waving. 'Thanks!'

'Yer welcome, maid.' The man nodded to them. 'Mind ye, I dunno she'll be wantin' ter take in any more lodgers.'

Fee frowned. 'Oh. I see.'

'But ask 'er anyways. She might 'ave some suggestions for ye.' The old man smiled kindly. 'Take care now.' He closed the window.

'Well, that's a good start.' Fee rolled her eyes. 'Come on. I'll buy you an ice cream.'

'Maybe we should just leave Marilyn here.' Ellie led the way back up the pretty cobblestone pathway, which was surrounded by wildflowers. They re-joined the street, and turned back towards the cove, making their way to an ice-cream van Fee had spotted on her previous walk into the village. 'Obviously, I have to get her repaired. Particularly if I want to sell her anyway. But we could... I dunno. Hire a car and carry on, and then come back for Marilyn at the end.'

They ordered ice creams from the cheery woman in the ice-cream van: Ellie chose raspberry ripple, and Fee chose chocolate.

They sat down on the edge of a wall to eat their ice creams, dangling their legs above the rocks below, where the beach started. A couple of cars sat parked on the road behind them; Ellie guessed they belonged to the dog walkers she could see on the beach.

'I think I've put on at least ten pounds since the operation.' Ellie savoured the rich creaminess of the ice cream on her tongue. 'God knows how I'm going to get back into all my work clothes.'

'Well, you look good. Better than before, if I'm honest,' Fee answered, shading her face from the sun with her hand. 'You were always so scrawny. Your cheeks have filled out. Do you good to get some meat on your bones.'

'No thanks.' Ellie made a face. Fee always looked lovely, she had to admit, and she was probably a size 16. Her friend had all the bombshell curves: the boobs, the bum and the little waist, wore dresses that showed off her lovely figure and wore her light auburn hair in a sharp bob. But Ellie knew, for herself, that she didn't have the confidence to get any bigger than she was. It wasn't that she thought being heavier was ugly. It was more that she had always felt the need to restrict herself. To stay small, narrow and under the radar.

Fee was sexy, partly because of the way she looked but partly also because she was confident about her body. She'd walk into a bar and get admiring looks from men and women. Ellie had never wanted that attention. She was afraid of it. She was afraid of being seen, because, in her mind, that made her exposed and vulnerable. So, she had always dieted and exercised and bound her physical self in tight, non-negotiable expectations of thinness.

Thinness was what her work expected, what her friends demanded, without actually saying it; what the designer dresses she bought asked for and what she, herself, wore as a camouflage.

'Why not? Women are supposed to have curves. I mean, fair enough if you're naturally athletic. But you and I both know that you hardly ever used to eat. I've seen you eat more in the past four days than I think I've seen you eat in the whole time I've known you.' Fee licked her ice cream. 'God, that's good.'

'I am enjoying the food, I have to admit.' Ellie assessed the ice cream in her hand. 'It feels as though... I don't know. Having the lump, it's been a bit of a wake-up call. And I'm just ravenous all the time. I could eat both of these and then some chips and not even think about it.'

'Well, you should!' Fee laughed. 'Hey. D'you think Esther Christie's one of them?' She pointed to the sea, where a group of women in bathing suits, some with swimming caps, were wading out of the water. They made their way back to a heap of bags and started to towel themselves off, talking and joking. There were six of them in all, and watching them gave Ellie a sense of longing. They seemed to be enjoying themselves so much.

She wondered if she would ever be brave enough to get into a swimming costume again. The way she felt at the moment, she doubted it.

'Come on. Let's go and see if one of them's Esther.' Fee stood up and held out a hand to Ellie.

'The man with the beard said she might not want a lodger,' Ellie protested.

'Well, then, we can still have a walk on the beach.' Fee raised her eyebrow at her friend. 'Come on.'

'Fine,' Ellie agreed. 'But I still think we should hire a car.'

They walked down the beach to the group of women.

'Hi there.' Fee waved as they got closer. 'Is one of you Esther Christie, by any chance?'

'Afternoon.' One of the women looked up. She had a blue towel knotted around her waist and long grey hair in a bun on her head. She wore a yellow T-shirt that read: I'VE BEEN TO THE SHIPWRECK AND SMUGGLING MUSEUM AT MAGPIE COVE. 'I'm Esther. Can I 'elp you, my love?'

'Ah. Hello, I'm Fiona, this is my friend, Ellie. Mark Gardner's fixing our motorhome at the moment and he said you might know of somewhere we could stay while he does it. He says he thinks it'll be a couple of weeks.'

'Oh, I see. I'm afraid I can't 'elp yer, though. I do usually 'ave a room for payin' guests, but I'm in a bit of a tizz at the moment with decorators everywhere. 'Avin a new kitchen put in, an' everythin' done up.'

'Not to worry,' Ellie interrupted. 'We were also thinking about hiring a car and heading off for a couple of weeks while the work gets done. Do any of you know where we could hire something?'

The women exchanged glances.

'Well, you'd be able to hire something in St Ives, I expect.' A woman about Ellie's age with short black hair and a red bathing suit answered. 'But we don't have an official car hire here. Though, if you've found Mark, you could ask him.' She gave Fee and Ellie a thoughtful look. 'However, if you're looking for somewhere to stay, I own the beach house there. It's free at the moment, if you're interested? I had a short let fall through.'

'That place?' Ellie pointed at the smart beach house on the cove. It was a good size, and featured a long, covered porch all along one side. Hanging baskets swayed gently in the light breeze coming off the sea and two rocking chairs sat outside. Ellie imagined herself sitting on one of them, looking out over the side of the beach where shingle gave way to white sand, watching the sun set. It was a nice image.

'Four bedrooms, but I've got one set up as an office at the moment. All mod cons. Come and have a look now, if you want.' The woman pulled on some tracksuit bottoms and zipped up a long-sleeved top. 'I'm Mara, by the way.'

'Well, only if it's convenient.' Ellie waved shyly to the rest of the group. 'We wouldn't want to interrupt anything.'

'No interruption. Just our weekly swim.' Mara grinned.

'All right, then.'

The beach house was gorgeous, Ellie had to admit. It could easily have been featured in a home décor magazine, or on one of the endless aspirational holiday home programmes she'd been watching recently. The wide, white-painted wood front door opened onto a spacious living room with original stripped pine floorboards, where two white sofas sat on a Turkish-style woven rug in washed-out blue and brown tones. A log burner sat in the middle of one wall; Ellie could imagine how cosy it would be in there in the winter. She liked the blue-patterned tiles that coved the interior of the fireplace in which it stood.

Two simple, stylish brass standard lamps stood against the rustic white walls. A large oil painting of a choppy sea scene framed in a burnished gold frame hung on one wall, and a pair of tall, ornate candlesticks with thick white candles stood on top of the mantelpiece.

Instead of the wooden floorboards, the kitchen was tiled with square terracotta tiles. A smart black Aga sat against the light grey stone and whitewashed wood-panelled walls, against which nestled various shiny silver appliances. Ellie was pleasantly surprised to see a top-of-the range coffee maker there.

'This is beautiful,' Fee breathed, taking it all in. 'How long have you had this place?'

'A few years now. I inherited it from my mum, but it was pretty down-at-heel then. My partner and I renovated it. That's how we met, actually.' Mara adjusted the stone-coloured throw that was folded neatly over one arm of the sofa. 'We lived in it for a while, but we've just moved into a new place in the village – we built it from scratch, this time. Still, I'll always love this place.' She smiled mistily, looking out of the window to the sea beyond. 'It's got a lot of history.'

'Can we look upstairs?' Fee asked.

'Oh, sure. Help yourself. I'll put the kettle on in the meantime.' Mara waved them towards the staircase.

The first bedroom they came to at the top of the stairs featured white-painted walls and a scrubbed pine wood floor, the same as downstairs. The space felt clean and fresh. Ellie sat on the king-size bed, admiring the dull gold antique bedframe and the thick white cotton sheets, completely plain apart from a small broderie anglaise pattern. The only other adornment in the room was a white pottery bowl full of grey-black pebbles. It sat on a table underneath the window opposite her, which faced the sea.

'Imagine waking up here every day,' Fee breathed, lying next to her on the bed.

'Hmm,' Ellie replied, non-committally.

'Come on. You have to admit this place is gorgeous. You couldn't ask for a nicer location. It's the height of summer. Do you really want to be trapped in some little car, driving around, when you could be here, relaxing? And I'm not convinced driving around in a cramped runaround is really a great idea. The motorhome was one thing: you could go and flake out in the back if you needed to. But this... this is really nice, Ellie. Maybe it's fate that Marilyn broke down here.' Fee rolled to face her friend.

'Maybe. Let's look at the rest of it before we make any wild decisions, though.' Ellie yawned. The bed was really comfortable.

The two other bedrooms were equally as lovely as the first; Fee claimed the second, which had a window facing the cove and another king-size bed, complete with a pink chaise longue. The third bedroom contained two single beds and could have been a children's room, even though it was still as impeccably designed as the rest. The fourth bedroom was a comfy office with a gorgeous vintage wooden desk and leather chair, as well as a sofa and plenty of shelving.

'See, I could work from here, babes. You could recuperate. We can cook, drink wine, have walks on the beach. I can't imagine what could be nicer.' Fee looked around happily. 'As long as there's decent internet connection, that is.'

'That bed was pretty comfy,' Ellie conceded. She knew Fee was right, and she didn't really know why she was being so fussy about the idea. Most people would love to stay in this lovely beach house for a couple of weeks. 'But... I suppose I got the idea of the tour in my head. At least it felt like I was... being productive on my time off. That I'd have something to show for it when I got back to work.'

Fee sighed. 'I know it's not what we planned, but stuff happens. Best laid plans and all that. And, newsflash: you don't have to be "productive" on holiday, Ellie.'

'Believe me, I know "stuff happens",' Ellie snapped. 'But what's the point of buying a bloody ridiculous motorhome if we don't get to at least go on a road trip?'

'I know.' Fee took Ellie's hand gently. 'But you have to give your body time to heal, Ellie. You've had a major operation. I really think you could get your head straight here if you just gave it a chance.'

Ellie shrugged. 'Fine. Okay.'

'Okay? That's a yes?' Fee whooped. 'Yesss!'

'Providing Mara has it free for a couple of weeks at least.' Ellie gave her friend a begrudging grin. 'You're right. I don't really want to live in a car for weeks. This place would be nicer.'

'Tea's ready if you want some.' Mara popped her head in at the door. 'So, what d'you think?'

'We'd like to take it, if you have it free for a couple of weeks?' Ellie asked, politely. 'I'm not sure how long the motorhome will take to be repaired, and I guess we're here until that happens. Or until I go back to work. That's maybe three weeks. Four, tops.'

'I have it free for a month or so, so that works.' Mara named the weekly rent, which seemed pretty reasonable to Ellie. But then, she remembered, she was used to paying exorbitant London prices, after all. 'That okay for you?'

Ellie nodded. 'No problem.'

'You said it had quite a history.' Fee ran her hand across the wooden mantelpiece in the study. 'Not haunted, is it? It's just that I don't want to wake up with a spectral Tudor milkmaid folding sheets at the end of the bed.' She caught Ellie's eye. 'What? You never know.'

'No, it's not haunted. As far as I know, anyway.' Mara laughed. 'I just meant, I inherited the place from my mum.'

'Oh, right. You did mention that.' Fee peered out of the window. 'Fabulous view.'

'I never knew she owned it until she died.' Mara leaned against the high-backed chair that sat next to the desk. 'She grew up here, then ran away as a teenager when she got pregnant with me. I've never known who my biological father was.' She stared at the desk for a few long moments. 'Anyway. Sorry. Not sure why I blurted that out.' She looked embarrassed.

'That's all right. Sounds tough,' Ellie replied, feeling the mood shift in the room.

'It was. Is still, sometimes. But on the other hand, this house will always be the thing that brought Brian and me together. My partner. The love of my life, really, apart from my kids, of course. So, it's very close to my heart.' Mara's face lit up, and her mention of Brian chased away the clouds in her eyes.

'As long as it's not haunted, you've got yourself a deal.' Ellie could see that Fee was already imagining herself sitting at the desk with her laptop.

Mara spoke softly. 'No ghosts. Just some unanswered questions for me.'

'Oh. Well, in that case, can we move in today? It's just that otherwise it's another night in the motorhome and I don't think Mark wants us at his garage overnight again. Plus, I think Marilyn's water tank's pretty low.' Fee exchanged looks with Ellie. 'That okay with you, babes?'

'Okay with me.' Ellie looked around her. It was a pleasant place. She could stay here.

'Don't see why not.' Mara looked at her phone. 'Can you give me a couple of hours to sort out a few things for you? I'd need to bring down some fresh towels, get some milk and bread in for you, that kind of thing.'

'That sounds great.' Fee jumped up and down on the spot, excitedly. 'I can't wait! This trip is turning out to be really fun.'

'I could do with that cup of tea.' Ellie smiled affectionately at her friend. 'But, yeah. Let's see what happens.'

SIX

'So, if we can leave Marilyn with you, then we'll be staying at the beach house,' Ellie explained to Mark as he sipped a cup of tea, standing in the yard next to her motorhome. She noticed his hands were covered in what looked like oil. *Par for the course for a mechanic*, she supposed: she wondered if they ever really got clean. Still, he had neatly trimmed fingernails.

In fact, once you looked past the overalls, scuffed work boots and slightly unruly blond hair, you could see that Mark Gardner was blessed with natural good looks. Ellie thought, just as she had when she'd first met him, that he had the kind of square jaw and good bone structure that could have earned him a place in a feature film, had he lived another life, somewhere other than Magpie Cove. He moved easily, like a cat; there was a kind of grace in his movements. Ellie wondered again if he worked out, or maybe did martial arts.

She realised she had trailed off from the conversation, and cleared her throat. He was looking at her expectantly; she realised he'd said something and she hadn't been listening.

'Sorry. What was that?' Mortified, she realised she was

blushing. She felt like she'd been caught red-handed, looking Mark over as if she were assessing a new pair of designer shoes.

'I said, I'll pop over and give you an update in a few days.' He gave her a half-smile. 'Now that I know where you are, like.'

'Right. Yes. Okay.' She tried to assume a business-like air. 'I'll leave you my mobile number as well. If it's useful.'

'Right you are,' was his taciturn reply.

Ellie scrambled in her bag for a pen and a piece of paper. As she did so, there was a commotion at the gate and two small children burst into the repair yard.

'Markee! Markee!' the little girl yelled, running up to him and hugging his legs. 'I got Star of the Week at school! For my colouring-in!'

'Hey, rascal! Let me put my cuppa down. Or I'll spill it all over your head, 'ere.' He grumbled good-naturedly at the little girl, whose light brown hair was cut into a bob, the fringe slightly in her eyes. He held the cup out to Ellie. ''Ere. Would you mind? She likely won't let go till I pick her up, will you, you menace?' he appealed to the girl, who was staring up at him devotedly.

'Sure, of course,' Ellie mumbled, taking it and watching as Mark swung the little girl effortlessly up into his arms, giving her an affectionate hug.

The boy who had accompanied his sister into the yard looked a little older than her – he was perhaps seven or eight, and she seemed more like five or six. They were dressed in school uniform, though on both of them it was rather askew, and in the boy's case, the knees of his trousers were scuffed.

It figured that a man like Mark would be a father, Ellie thought, but her heart sank just a little. She berated herself instantly for the feeling, which was genuinely ridiculous. Mark was just an unusually good-looking Cornish mechanic she'd met precisely one day ago. It wasn't like he'd asked her to marry him.

If anything, Ellie realised that what she was actually experiencing was a reality check about meeting a new man in general, at her age, after having had a mastectomy. What was the statistic – that you were more likely to be hit by lightning than get married after you were forty, or something like that? Granted, she was thirty-seven, but forty wasn't far away. Of course Mark Gardner was married with kids. And even if he wasn't, neither he nor any man would want her.

'All right, Danny? How was school?' Mark reached out and ruffled the boy's hair. Danny shrugged. 'Same.'

'Where's your mum?' Mark asked, looking towards the gates. 'Oh, 'ere she is.'

A woman with blonde hair up in a ponytail, wearing a pink vest and matching jogging bottoms, and holding what looked like a jewel-encrusted phone, waved as she followed her son in. She was talking to someone, holding the phone flat in front of her; Ellie could hear the other person – a man – on speakerphone.

In fact, the woman seemed to be having an argument with the man at the other end. Mark and Ellie exchanged a glance.

'Kids, look at this big motorhome! It belongs to Ellie, 'ere. I think if we ask 'er really nicely, she'll let us have a look inside. What d'you think?' Mark raised his eyebrows at Ellie, and she knew that he was trying to create a diversion from the woman – Ellie guessed she was his partner – arguing on the phone.

'Sure!' Ellie replied, brightly. 'You guys can sit in the driver's seat if you like.'

'Has it got a toilet?' Danny asked, seriously. 'Because you can't go on holiday without going to the toilet, you know.'

Ellie laughed, surprised at the serious question. She wasn't really around children very much, but she'd always liked them.

'It does have a toilet,' she confirmed.

'Okay, let's go, then!' Mark herded them towards Marilyn and opened the door. The kids climbed in and Ellie followed.

'Thanks,' Mark murmured. 'Sorry about this. My sister's

goin' through some ups and downs with her fella at the moment, and I don't like them to have to listen to it.'

'Your sister? I thought they were your kids,' Ellie replied, as the two little ones raced off into Marilyn's interior.

'Oh! No. I'm their uncle.' He closed the door behind them. 'Amber's five and Danny's eight. My sister Jamey's been on and off with their dad over the years. They're together at the moment, but it kind of... goes up and down, if you know what I mean.' He gave her a rueful smile. 'I look after 'em when I can, give 'er a bit of head space, or quality time with Darren. They're great kids, but kids aren't exactly helpful if you're tryin' to rebuild a relationship.'

'Right. I guess not.' Ellie glanced up at the end bedroom where she could see Amber jumping enthusiastically on the bed, with Danny watching on. 'You don't have any of your own?'

'No,' he answered, shortly.

Ellie felt it would be rude to ask if he was single at this point, and anyway, it was none of her business. Though, if he was, she suspected that he wouldn't stay that way for long. Surely there were far too many single women in their late thirties and early forties who had heard that stupid, probably made-up statistic about getting married when you were over forty, and would likely beat each other to death with their spinsters' brooms to get hold of an attractive single man of the same age.

'You got kids?' Mark asked, casually.

'Me? No.' Ellie instinctively crossed her arms protectively across her chest. He shot her a curious look, but said nothing. 'I mean... never got around to it, I suppose. I'm a lawyer. Work kind of takes up most of my time.'

'Oh, like, in court? D'you wear a wig an' a gown?' he asked, a twinkle in his eye.

'No! Dresses, mostly. I work in a law firm.'

'You must be brainy, then. Lot of book learnin',' he added.

'I suppose so.' She thought about her years of study. 'A lot of books, yes.' She wanted to add *and not much else*, but she stopped herself.

'Not much of that in the car trade.' He shrugged. 'Mind you, I do like readin'. Keeps the brain active.'

'Well, I couldn't do what you do. It must take a lot of expertise to be able to look at an engine and understand what it does. Never mind knowing how to repair it.'

'Take things apart and put 'em back together again.' He ran his hand over the kitchen work surface near where they stood. 'That's pretty much all there is to it. I like findin' solutions. And I love old girls like this one.' He tapped one of the cupboards above the kitchen area. 'Don't make 'em like that anymore, I tell you.'

'That's why we call her Marilyn, me and Fee.' Ellie laughed. 'She's all curves and old-fashioned glamour. Well, 80s glamour, anyway. Maybe we should have called her Madonna or something.'

'Lot of the 50s in the 80s – design-wise,' Mark said. 'Either way, 'twas a great time for gas guzzlers.'

'Sorry about that, hun. Darren's off on one again.' Jamey stepped up into the berth and looked around at Marilyn's interior. 'Wow! I love this! You working on it, are you, Mark?'

'Yeah. It's Ellie's.' Mark held out a hand to Ellie as if to introduce her. 'Ellie, this is my sister, Jamey.'

'Hi, Jamey. Nice to meet you.' Ellie could see the resemblance between them, now that they were next to each other. Jamey had the same direct blue eyes and good bone structure, but there was something more restless about her. She didn't have Mark's stability, somehow.

'Likewise. Mark, can you give the kids their tea? Darren wants me to meet him at the pub.' She darted a glance to her phone. Ellie thought, for a brief moment, that Jamey seemed panicked. 'I'll only be a couple of hours, okay?'

'All right. I'll take 'em to the café, then. But I've got another couple of hours' work to do.'

Amber and Danny reappeared from the bedroom.

'Found the toilet?' Ellie asked Danny, trying not to laugh. He looked as serious as before. 'What did you think of it?'

'It's very clean,' he replied, after some thought.

'Oh. Well, that's good.' Ellie matched his serious expression. 'What you want from a toilet, really.'

'Mum, there's a shower and it really works! And a fridge!' Amber squealed. 'It's like my Barbie camper. But bigger.'

'That's nice, sweetheart,' Jamey answered, looking at her phone. 'Okay. I'll see you guys later. Uncle Mark's going to take you to the café for tea.' She kissed both children and waved. 'Nice to meet you, Ellie,' she added. 'See you later, hun.'

Jamey pecked Mark on the cheek and jumped down into the yard, not bothering to use Marilyn's steps.

Mark sighed. 'Looks like I've got two little 'elpers again today, then.' He smiled distractedly at the children. 'Come on, trouble. Let's get you a drink.' He picked up Amber from where she'd climbed up into the driver's seat. Danny sat in the passenger seat, staring out at the yard.

'Come on, Dan,' Mark repeated. 'Let's go.' He turned to Ellie. 'I'll let you get your stuff out and all that. Catch up in a few days about the repairs, okay?'

'Of course. You've got your hands full.' Ellie looked around, thinking about what she'd need to take to the beach house. Fee would be back in a minute from the shops, and they'd take what they could carry for now. 'See you later.'

She stood at the window for a moment, watching Mark shepherd the children across the yard and towards the office. He clearly took care of them often. Ellie wondered why an attractive, caring man like Mark – with his own business, no less – didn't have a family of his own.

But then again, she'd been asked the same question herself

many times. She always said it was because of her work, but was it really? Or had she deliberately chosen a career that left little time for love and family, providing a perfect excuse?

And if that was the case, why?

There were answers to those questions, but she didn't want to think about them now.

She turned away from the window and started packing. There would be time enough at the beach house for introspection, not that she planned to give herself any more time to think than she ever had. Thinking often led Ellie to places she would rather not return to.

SEVEN

Dawn broke pretty early at this time of year, Ellie realised, as she lay in bed and stared groggily at the crack in the curtains, through which a shaft of sunlight streamed straight into her eyes. She lay under the duvet for a few minutes, listening to the seagulls out on the cove. As well as their seasidey squawks, the shushing of the waves on the sand was beautifully lulling.

After a while, Ellie realised that she could hear faint voices on the beach, and went to her window to look out. Blearily, she rubbed her eyes and recognised the same group of wild swimmers – Mara's group, she thought, unless there was another troupe who wore brightly coloured swimming caps.

Ellie padded downstairs and made herself a cup of tea, and took it out onto the porch, wrapping her fleecy robe around her. She settled into one of the rocking chairs and sipped the tea, taking in the early morning air. The breeze coming in off the sea was so clean and energising she breathed it in as if it was medicine, sipping her tea.

Her phone buzzed; she tilted the screen towards her to read the message and was surprised to see it was from her friend, Toni.

Hey. Hope you're okay. Called for you at the flat but you weren't around. Let me know if you're around next week for a catch up.

In fact, Ellie had been so focused on the road trip, she'd forgotten to let any of her friends know that she was going; not that they seemed to care. She frowned, thinking about how to reply.

Fine, thanks. Have gone away for a few weeks to recover. Catch up when I get home?

Ellie pressed Send and watched the screen for a reply from Toni.

Spa break? Enjoy!

Ellie stared thoughtfully out to sea. If Toni thought that cancer was nothing more than a great excuse to spend time in a hot tub, then she wasn't sure she wanted to see her anyway. What was it about people not understanding what she was going through?

As she stared out onto the sea, Ellie watched the women swimming, stopping to tread water and chat and laugh. What fun they seemed to be having, and what a great way to start the day a dip in the sea must be. She'd swum in the sea plenty of times over the years, but not in Cornwall, and not so early in the day. It would be much colder than the Mediterranean holidays she was used to.

For a few years, she'd gone along on one of the big group holidays to which the senior partner in her law firm invited all his favourites. It had been on a yacht in Sardinia, and she had dived from the boat into the turquoise water, the sun on her shoulders. None of those company holidays was really relaxing, because Ellie was always worrying about saying the wrong thing or keeping up with everyone else, whether that meant drinking games, poker or taking part in all the activities that were organised: wine tasting, jet-skiing, hiking in the hills. But for those brief moments where she'd been alone, under the water, she had been happy.

Ellie reflected that it was, in fact, completely nuts to have gone on so many exotic holidays and not enjoyed any of them. She was actually enjoying sitting on the porch of the beach house and drinking a cup of tea more than she had enjoyed the endless bottles of champagne on the private yacht.

Well, that's messed up, she said to herself.

Some of the women were getting out of the water. One of them – Ellie thought it was Mara – waved to her, and she waved back. Gradually they all made their way out and stood there, laughing and chatting, getting changed under their towels and drinking from Thermos flasks.

Ellie watched them. She felt no need to go over; she was happy where she was, but it was nice nonetheless to feel that she was now an accepted part of the landscape in some small way.

The door opened and Fee came to stand next to her on the porch, also dressed in pyjamas and her robe.

'Wow. I had the most amazing sleep, babes. You okay?' She rubbed Ellie's shoulder gently. 'I hope your bed was half as comfy as mine. Didn't want to get up, but I've got a call in an hour.' She yawned. 'Fancy some breakfast?'

'That would be great.' Ellie drained her mug. 'Yeah, I slept like a log, actually. Chest feels a bit less sore too. So far, anyway.'

'Awesome. See, I told you the beach house would be good for you.' Fee took in a lungful of the sea air. 'Good for me too, I reckon. God, it's going to be hard to go back to smoggy old London after this.'

'Let's not think about that for now,' Ellie advised. 'I think we should have pancakes.'

'Pancakes it is,' Fee called over her shoulder, walking to the kitchen.

Fee was chatting animatedly to one of her design clients on a Zoom call when Ellie left the beach house, having decided to explore Magpie Cove. Fee put herself on mute briefly to call out that Ellie *had* to pay a visit to the village café – and, ideally, bring her back some lunch.

It was the first time in a long time – maybe forever – that Ellie remembered being at a loose end and completely alone. *I can do whatever I want!* she thought, gleefully. There was no one pinging her with urgent work messages on her phone, no clients to call, no paperwork to be done, and certainly no loud, demanding group of lawyers in Speedos challenging each other to down as many Jager Bombs as possible.

The wild swimmers were gone now, and apart from a woman walking her dog, Ellie had the beach to herself. If it was still term time, which it must be, given that Mark's niece and nephew had arrived in school uniform with their mum the day before, then Ellie supposed Magpie Cove wouldn't start to get really touristy for another few weeks.

The cove itself was smallish, but beautiful, filled with fine golden sand for the most part, bordered by piles of black boulders that looked like they had tumbled there from the hands of a giant. The craggy cliffs that rose up around it on the right, like a shield, gave Ellie a twinge of vertigo as she shaded her eyes with her hand and gazed up to their summit. She'd always heard that Cornwall was romantic, and now she could see why. There was something wild and magical about the turquoise sea and the grey-black cliffs that hinted at the shadows of caves under the tide line. Ellie wondered if this was one of those places that held legends of smugglers.

The cluster of fishing boats moored up around a small harbour master's hut brought back a forgotten memory: a seaside holiday she had had as a child, before her parents had split up. She didn't remember where it was. All she remembered was holding her dad's hand as they walked around a fishing harbour, looking at the crabs and the lobsters in nets. She had been happy then.

She stopped for a moment, surprised at the sudden lump in her throat.

One forgotten moment, so long ago.

She hadn't thought about her dad in a long time. In fact, she hadn't seen him for about five years. Occasionally he would come back from Spain with his wife for a visit and Ellie would meet them for a drink or a meal. There would be a polite conversation, catching up on the holidays they'd been on, how work was going for Ellie, how the house in Spain was. But that was the extent of their contact.

Not even after Ellie's mum had died had her dad stepped up or come to visit her more. He'd attended the funeral, and checked that Ellie was still living in university accommodation. He'd offered that she could come and stay with him and Gloria in Spain if she'd wanted, after graduation, but she hadn't wanted to: Ellie had got the distinct impression that if she'd stayed longer than a weekend, Gloria would have made her feel unwelcome.

Ellie wandered up to the stone steps that led up to a road bordering the beach and climbed them. A row of slightly dilapidated Victorian terraced houses faced out onto the beach on the other side of the road, and a sign indicated that a narrow lane led onto the high street. She followed it, smiling at a jogger as he passed by, and an elderly lady with a shopping trolley who gave her a friendly 'Good morning'.

Her chest was still sore, but she had more energy today. Still, she would take it easy. A coffee and maybe some cake at the café was a good place to start – especially if it was as nice as Fee had said it was.

Ellie turned onto the small high street, walking past the Shipwreck and Smuggling Museum. She thought about going in, but the promise of coffee was too attractive.

A tinkle of bells accompanied Ellie's entry to Serafina's Café; she noticed a string of small brass bells on a colourful string attached to the inside of the wooden door, which had large glass panels. The front of the café was also glass-panelled, meaning that she had been able to see into its cosy interior.

Inside, two elderly ladies sat at a corner table; a young family occupied a leather sofa nearby; and three women were having an animated conversation, lounging in easy chairs with their coffees. Fleetwood Mac played in the background, and the chocolatey smell of freshly ground coffee filled the air. Ellie's stomach grumbled. She didn't know why: she'd only just had breakfast, but apparently the sea air was doing something to her.

She approached the counter, eyes widening at the huge cakes that sat on the counter under glass domes.

'All vegan, would you believe.' The woman behind the counter smiled at her, adjusting her apron. 'Made over the road at Maude's Fine Buns. And we have a selection of individual patisserie too.' She pointed to a tray of very professional-looking iced custard slices and *mille feuille*. 'Otherwise, we've got a lush brunch menu today. Eggs Florentine, pancakes, bacon, you name it.' She pointed at a chalk board behind her that listed the menu. 'Different every day.'

'Wow. I don't know what to choose.' Ellie stared at the board. 'I mean... I have had breakfast already, so I probably don't need brunch.'

'Never mind needing it. Do you fancy it? I love the eggs

Florentine myself.' The woman laughed. 'And it's pay-what-you-can, too. I don't think I've seen you in here before, right?'

'No, we just got here. My friend and I are staying in the beach house for a week or two until our motorhome gets fixed,' Ellie explained. 'Okay. I think I've decided. Can I have a flat white, the pancakes and bacon?'

'Of course you can! I'll bring it to you.' The woman gestured around the café. 'Sit anywhere. It'll just be a few minutes. You're staying at Mara's place, then?'

'The one on the cove, yeah,' Ellie replied.

'Oh, it's lovely. Magpie Cove's good for the soul. I'm Lila, by the way.'

'Ellie.'

Lila reached over the counter and handed Ellie her coffee. 'Go on and find a seat, I'll bring the rest.'

Good for the soul. She didn't feel like her soul had received much attention over the years. She wasn't religious. She wasn't 'spiritual' in the way that some of her friends described themselves, doing yoga and meditation and vegan retreats in Goa. She wouldn't have known where to start.

She sat down in a brown velvet easy chair which had a comfy tapestry cushion resting against the arm. Maybe what her soul needed was a break. In which case, she was having one.

Box ticked.

After brunch – which was completely delicious, and left Ellie feeling stuffed – she wandered up the high street, looking in the windows and enjoying not having anywhere to be.

She admired the small independent butcher's shop, and bought some sausages for her and Fee's dinner, plus, on a whim, a leg of lamb that she thought they could slow roast in the Aga. On special occasions, Ellie's mum would make her famous roast lamb, and Ellie remembered how to do it: turn the oven up full, rub the lamb in olive oil, salt and pepper, lie it on a bed of garlic cloves and rosemary (with the same on top), cover it with foil, put it in the oven and immediately turn the temperature down, then leave it for four hours.

It was a simple recipe, but it always came out perfectly. As a child, Ellie remembered begging her mother to make her special lamb more often, but it was only as an adult that she realised that lamb was expensive, and her mum probably couldn't afford have afforded to buy it very often.

She had overpaid for brunch in the café, remembering that it was a pay-what-you-can community café, and mindful that there would likely be many patrons who couldn't afford to pay much at all. Ellie lived a high-flying lifestyle now, but she had never forgotten where she'd come from, and she could see, walking around, that Magpie Cove had plenty of families that didn't have much. Despite that, it seemed to be a happy place, where people stopped to chat in the street and looked out for each other.

Next, she called in at the antiques shop and browsed happily among the candlesticks and the foxed mirrors, imagining buying some pieces for her flat. Generally, her taste was modern and sleek, but there were some things that caught her eye: a vintage crystal chandelier and a high-backed mahogany chair with elaborate carvings on the back. The owner, a bearded man about her age in a faded band T-shirt and bottle-green cardigan – despite the glorious weather – told her that he had recently inherited the shop from his grandfather and had decided to reopen it. Ellie took his card: perhaps she would come back for the chandelier if she was feeling daring.

She wandered back along the high street, taking in the sights and smells of the village. It was late lunchtime before she remembered that she had promised to bring some lunch back for Fee, and rushed back into the café to get something.

'Hey! You almost 'ad me over there.' Mark Gardner held out a hand to protect Ellie from knocking his coffee out of his grip. He was standing just inside the door of the café.

'Oh, God, I'm so sorry,' Ellie apologised, mortified.

'No 'arm done.' He nodded, and they looked at each other slightly awkwardly for a moment.

'Just come to get some lunch for Fee,' she explained, wanting to fill the silence.

'Ah. Right,' he replied.

Fortunately, Lila passed them, at that moment, carrying a tray. 'Oh, hi, Mark! I don't know if you know, but it's my birthday tomorrow. I'm having drinks at The Lookout from about seven. You should come along! And you, Ellie. Bring your friend too.'

'Oh, I wouldn't want to intrude,' Ellie excused herself, quickly. 'We're just visitors, really.'

'No trouble. The more the merrier!' Lila trilled. 'I want to look popular, after all.'

'Well, we might. Thanks.' Ellie felt a little self-conscious about being asked. She didn't know why – perhaps it was that she was still on London settings, where strangers or neighbours never spoke to you, let alone asked you to birthday parties.

'You'll come, won't you, Mark?' Lila probed. 'Go on. Live a little.'

'Depends. Try to come, though. Ta.' Mark flashed Lila a shy smile. Ellie caught herself thinking that he did have a lovely smile, though it was pretty infrequent from what she'd seen so far.

Ellie cleared her throat. 'So. How's it going with Marilyn?'

'Not too bad. One of the parts come in, waitin' for the rest.' He had a nice voice too, Ellie thought: deep, but with that pleasant Cornish burr.

'Oh. All right. Well, let me know if you need me for anything. You know, operating a jack. Doing an oil change. That kind of thing,' she joked, instantly feeling her words land as flat as a pancake, as Mark just looked confused.

'You a mechanic, are you?' he asked, seriously. Now Ellie

felt that it looked like she was making fun of him, when she wasn't: it had just been a joke, but now it had gone horribly wrong.

'Oh. No. Just joking,' she said with a shrug, wishing he would just disappear. A table of teenagers nearby was watching them, whispering and giggling to each other. Ellie had no doubt that she and Mark were being made fun of.

She smiled, politely. 'Well, I should let you go.'

'Right you are.' Mark looked away, uncomfortably, and made for the door, stepping into the same space as she did, meaning that they accidentally bumped into each other again.

Oh, for the love of... Ellie remonstrated with herself. The table of teenagers laughed openly this time.

'Right. See you, then,' he muttered, and practically bounded out of the café.

Ellie, ignoring the teens, made it back to the counter and asked Lila what she had left for takeaway lunch options. The teens were probably quite nice, but had obviously found the whole awkward exchange brilliantly amusing. *As it probably was*, she thought as she waited for Lila to portion up some quiche and a salad for Fee. Why had she felt so awkward? *Perhaps it was his terrible social skills*, she thought. It was always awkward talking to people who weren't skilled in keeping a conversation going. He'd been positively sociable the other day when they were alone in the motorhome, but today he didn't seem to want to chat.

Her awkwardness with Mark was definitely nothing to do with the fact that he was breathtakingly gorgeous. Ellie chided herself for having the thought – objectifying the poor man – but he really did have those movie-star good looks, and even though Ellie had never seen Mark wearing anything other than dirty coveralls and muddy work boots, he was still very attractive. Today, her gaze had been drawn to his forearms again, as he'd been wearing a plain white T-shirt and a pair of jeans that showed off his tanned muscles. There was something very sexy about some men's forearms, though she couldn't explain exactly what it was.

She imagined kissing those slightly pouty lips, and a shiver of excitement caught her off guard. *Oh God*, she thought, *I've become some kind of walking cliché.* Had the operation done something to her mind? Was this a side effect of breast cancer recovery that no one ever talked about: lusting after hot but monosyllabic mechanics?

Come on, Ellie. That's not exactly revolutionary, she berated herself. She wouldn't be the first woman to fancy a hot guy who fixed things, and she certainly wouldn't be the last. Still, she'd never considered someone like Mark to be her type.

She paid for Fee's lunch and took a slice of the chocolate cake home for both of them too, thanking Lila and promising to pop in again soon.

As she emerged back into the sunny street, her heart lifted unexpectedly. *Well, so what if I am a cliché?* she thought, suddenly. *An innocent little crush on someone isn't going to hurt me. It's not like anything is going to happen.*

Perhaps, now, after the operation, she cared a little less about what people thought. Perhaps, now, she knew that not everything was deadly serious.

Could it be that she was enjoying herself? Humming a tune under her breath, she walked back to the beach house, carrying the food. There was something lovely about not having any plans apart from eating chocolate cake for the rest of the day.

She was glad that they'd stayed in Magpie Cove, after all.

EIGHT

'Wow. Okay, this beats standing on the street outside a Soho bar.'

Fee and Ellie stood at the edge of the cliff, looking down onto the little coastal village of Morven. There was a waist-high fence a few feet before the edge, and large terracotta plant pots dotted the perimeter of the pub garden, planted with palm, bay and olive trees.

'It's lovely,' Ellie agreed. The view was stunning. Morven was the next coastal village along from Magpie Cove, and The Lookout pub sat on top of the cliff, with a view of the whole bay. The sea was flat and calm, bathed in a pink-violet light from the sun, which sat languorously on the horizon. 'Shall we go in?'

The party was under way already, it seemed, and people had spilled out into the garden, sipping champagne and cocktails in the warm evening. The clink of glasses and the hum of laughter and conversation filled the air. Through the wide, open bifold glass doors, the bar glittered with fairy lights that reflected their gold glow on the long steel bar. The weathered wooden tables held large vases of summer flowers: blowsy pink Cornish roses, creamy sweet peas and bold purple rhododendrons jostled with out-of-season lilacs. Their seductive scent hung in the air like the memory of a childhood in the Cornish countryside. It made Ellie want a house with a huge flower garden.

'You came!' Lila embraced Fee and Ellie in a hug, carrying a champagne glass. 'Sorry. I didn't spill on you, did I? I've done it twice to other people already.'

'You're fine!' Ellie grinned. 'Happy birthday! This is my friend, Fee.'

'Hi, Fee.' Lila kissed her on both cheeks. 'I get a bit affectionate when I'm tipsy,' she explained.

Fee laughed. 'No trouble at all. What a lovely night!'

'I know. I love it up here.' Ellie gazed out at the view, which, even from inside the bar, was remarkable. 'Anyway. My fella Nathan's here somewhere, I should introduce you. And there's a ton of food by the bar, just help yourselves!' She waved at a tall man with a mass of tumbling dark curls at the other side of the room who was beckoning to her. 'Nathan! Oh, he wants me to go over there. I'll be back! Enjoy!'

'Food?' Fee raised her eyebrow at Ellie.

'As if you had to ask.' Ellie followed her to the groaning table where what looked like an entire festival's food allocation had been arranged. By now, she had had to accept that her previous macrobiotic, vegan diet was a thing of the past, at least temporarily. Ellie was chagrined to admit that she hadn't been a vegan for particularly ethical reasons; it was more that her friends had recommended a particular diet on the basis of health, and she'd started it. Actually, Ellie knew that their recommendation was less health-based than coming from a desire to be thin. She had certainly been thin for many years, eating that way. But she had also been hungry.

Now, as she gazed at the table of salads, pies, tarts, crusty bread, pâté, cold meats, cheeses, pickles and chutneys, she felt a brief guilt, followed by a very hungry growl from her stomach.

She took a plate and began loading it up. The guilt was meaningless, she rationalised. Her body needing food to heal, on the other hand, was very meaningful.

'Look at the size of these!' Fee sighed happily as she stood alongside Ellie, spooning fat green marinated olives onto her plate. 'Oooh! Manchego!'

'Evenin'.' Mark approached the end of the food table, reaching for a plate just as Ellie reached for a bread roll. Her arm knocked his, making him drop his plate, but he managed to catch it before it hit the floor.

'Oh! Goodness! I'm so sorry!' Ellie had tried to catch the plate at the same time as Mark. He had kept his grip on it, and her hand had clutched his wrist by accident.

She let it go instantly, as if it was hot. 'You've got it. Right,' she muttered.

'Hello,' Mark repeated, smiling at her panicked reaction.

'Hello.' Ellie laughed nervously. Fee shot her an amused look. 'That was... sorry, I don't know what happened then.'

'I'm gonna let you finish choosin', I think.' He looked at the plate of rolls and back to her, clearly finding the whole episode funny. 'That bread roll's waitin'. Careful, now.'

'Watch out for those sausages,' Fee giggled. 'They might be slippery. You don't want to end up with one down your dress. Hi, Mark,' she grinned, before walking off and sitting down at a nearby table. *Don't leave me alone with him*, Ellie willed her friend, glaring at her, but Fee laughed and made a kissy face at her.

Not helpful.

'Well, that was embarrassing.' Ellie cleared her throat. 'So, how's things?'

'All right.' Mark cut a piece of deep-filled chicken and ham pie and put it on his plate, spooning on some Greek salad to go with it. 'How're you?'

'Fine. When I'm not throwing plates at people.'

'To be fair, I caught it. Disaster averted.' He shot a shy smile at her. 'How's the beach house?'

'Really nice. I love waking up to the sound of the waves in the cove.' Ellie broke a piece off the bread roll she had reached for and put it in her mouth. It was warm, yeasty and utterly delicious. She looked around for some butter. *In for a penny, in for a pound*, she thought. Until she and Fee had ended up in Magpie Cove, she hadn't eaten bread or butter for about ten years.

It was a revelation how good it was.

'Oh, God.' She moaned with pleasure, then caught the surprised expression on Mark's face. 'Oh. Sorry. It's just that this bread is really, really good.'

'You really like your food, then.' He was watching her with an amused look.

'I guess so. I didn't think I did. I don't think I've eaten this well, like, ever.' She chewed the bread thoughtfully. 'It's not just soft. It's nutty as well. Yeasty. The crust has so much flavour.'

Mark reached for a disc of local butter in a little foil wrapper that bore the name 'Gordon's'.

''Ere. To go with it.'

Ellie unwrapped the butter and spread it on the roll.

'Oh. My. God,' she murmured as she bit into it. 'I think I might have died and gone to heaven.'

'Best dairy in the south-west, Gordon's.' Mark grinned, watching her. 'Lots of people come to Cornwall for the food. I'm a bit of a cook myself, actually. When I gets the time.'

'You are? I can't cook. Well, I've never tried, to be honest,' Ellie confessed. 'Beyond the basics, anyway,'

'You should give it a go. Do a course or somethin'.'

'Maybe. I just don't ever have the time of that kind of thing, usually – what with work, and everything. I'd love to, though.'

'Well, I could teach you, while you're 'ere. If you wanted? Or not, whatever.' He separated a large piece of the pie with the edge of his fork and ate it, as if looking for a reason not to have to say anything else.

'Oh, I couldn't ask you to do that,' Ellie said, quickly.

'Happy to,' he said, swallowing. 'I got the weekend free if you want to come over. Make bread, if you want, since you like it so much.'

'Oh. Maybe. Thanks!' Ellie didn't quite know what to say. Was Mark asking her out on a date? She wasn't sure she was ready for that.

'Just as friends, like. I'm not asking you out, if that's the problem.' He seemed to know what she was thinking. 'I just like cookin', bakin', whatever. Be nice to 'ave a bit of company.'

'Oh. Well, in that case, okay,' Ellie finished eating the roll. *What the hell*, she thought. *What's the harm in making bread? And he'd said it wasn't a date. It definitely wasn't a date.* 'That would be really nice. Thank you.'

'Saturday? I might have to take Jamey's kids Sunday.' He glanced over at Fee, who had left her dinner on the table and was talking to a good-looking red-haired girl by the bar. 'Anyway, lemme know. You got my number. I'll let you get back to Fee.'

'Oh... yes, I should go and keep her company. Or... not,' Ellie added, realising that Fee and the girl were flirting. 'Anyway, I should sit down with all this food.'

'Right.' He grinned. 'You be careful, mind. Those plates can be deadly.'

Ellie rolled her eyes. 'Very funny. You're a comedian.'

'No one's ever called me a comedian before, but I'll take it.' He chuckled. 'See you Saturday.'

NINE

When he opened the door, Mark was wearing a red-and-white checked apron over jeans and a T-shirt. Aretha Franklin's voice belted towards Ellie from inside.

'Hi. I was just tidyin' up. Come in.' Mark stepped aside as Ellie entered the hallway. 'Leave your shoes 'ere if you want.'

The hallway was neat and tidy, and Ellie tried to mask her surprise that the whole wall on one side was covered with a purpose-built bookshelf stuffed with novels.

'You read a lot,' she said, then kicked herself for stating the obvious.

'Yeah. I'm on a crime kick at the mo. Used to be history. I try and read the big prize shortlists, but I don't always get the time.' He picked up a heavy hardback Ellie had seen advertised in magazines as one of the big literary hits of the year. 'This one almost beat me. Worth stickin' with it, though. You read it?'

'No. I don't read a lot of fiction,' she confessed. 'I work long hours, and when I get home I usually go to the gym or out with friends. I spend a lot of my day reading legal briefs, so it takes it out of you a bit.' Ellie kicked herself for not reading more important novels. Or any novels, come to that.

'Fair enough. You should, though. It's really good.' He put it back on the shelf. 'Come in, anyway,'

Ellie followed Mark through a winding hallway. The house was one of the terraces that overlooked the cove, and while some of them had been converted into flats, Mark's seemed to be just one house.

'So is all this yours?' she asked, looking around. A wide staircase led upstairs from the hallway which featured what looked like an original Victorian tiled floor. Everything was painted white.

'All mine. It's a four-bedroom house.' He led her into a surprisingly large, open-plan kitchen-diner which had obviously been extended: three large windows were built into the ceiling, and wide, floor-to-ceiling windows and doors led out onto the garden.

'It's lovely.' Ellie looked around at the state-of-the-art kitchen and fashionable décor.

'You didn't think someone like me 'ad a KitchenAid.' He observed her as she took in Mark's expensive gadgets.

'That's a really nice coffee machine,' she said. 'I've got the model before this one, at home. They're really expensive.'

'Good coffee's worth payin' for.' He grinned. 'Want one?'

'I'd love one, thanks.' Ellie went over to the sliding doors, which were open, and stepped into the garden. Clearly, running your own garage in Cornwall paid well. She didn't want to ask if all of this just came from whatever Mark had made in his business, or whether he'd had an inheritance, perhaps, but she was dying to.

'I'll bring it out,' he called.

Outside, the garden stretched easily a hundred feet long and about the same in width. Mature trees lined the edges alongside a high hedge, but there was still plenty of sun on the lawn, even though the garden was north-facing. A black rattan garden furniture set with cream cushions sat on a large deck overlooking the lawn. A profusion of summer flowers lined the beds on the right-hand side.

Ellie sat on one of the chairs and took it all in. You would never have known that any of this existed behind the façade of the terraces overlooking the beach. It was like its own little world out there: an English garden oasis. She took in a deep breath and let it out again. There was no noise except for bird-song and Mark's radio in the background. Peace entered her body, and she breathed it in again, gratefully.

'One coffee.' Mark stepped out onto the deck, holding a tray with two cups, a milk jug and a sugar bowl that held the rough-edged sugar cubes she knew were the premium kind, because she bought them too – one of the few sweet treats she'd ever allowed herself had been one cube in her coffee when she made one at home.

He set the tray down on the glass-topped table and sat down, allowing a space between them.

'Didn't know if you took sugar, or wanted it black. I frothed the milk,' he indicated the jug, 'if you want,'

'Thanks, Mark.' Ellie took the mug and added a sugar cube, then a splash of the milk. She sipped it. 'Aaagh. That's good,'

'I get the beans from Worthington's, in London,' he said. 'You probably know it. Best I've found.'

'I love Worthington's.' Ellie sipped her coffee again. 'I go to the one in Borough Market most weeks,'

'No way! I've always wanted to go.' He smiled at her over his mug.

'I'll take you, some time,' she said, without thinking. 'Oh. I mean... if you ever come to London.'

'I'd love that,' he said, quietly, his mouth turning up at one corner as he sipped his coffee.

There was a brief, comfortable silence, which Ellie broke by saying, 'Your garden is gorgeous, by the way.' It wasn't that she felt she needed to – it was actually nice, sitting quietly with Mark.

'Thanks.'

'It's so wide. And long.'

'Not the first time I've 'eard that.' He caught her eye; his had an unexpected twinkle in it.

Did Mark Gardner just make a smutty joke? Ellie snorted in surprise. 'Says you.'

'Ha. No, I bought the garden next door a few years ago. It 'ad its trees and all that in it already, though there was a bit of work getting it to what it is now. Glad I did.'

'It's beautiful. They're flats, then, next door?'

'Yeah. More affordable. The tenants are nice, so I don't mind if they wants to use the garden now an' again. One of the women does yoga 'ere sometimes. Another one paints, on sunny days.'

Ellie found herself feeling suddenly and illogically jealous of the women who got to hang out in Mark's garden, doing downward dog and painting the rhododendrons. Maybe Mark was some kind of local stud who had hordes of women on the go? She could believe it: it seemed highly unlikely that he wasn't engaged or married or at least in a relationship. Perhaps he preferred to play the field. That would explain a lot.

'That's nice of you,' she said, neutrally.

''T'aint nothin'.' He shrugged. 'So. You ready to make bread?'

'I think so.' Ellie finished her coffee. 'But I hope you understand that I am useless at this kind of thing.'

'Everyone's got to start somewhere.' He stood up, and picked up the tray. 'After you.'

'Let's do it.' Ellie's stomach rumbled. 'Oh. I might need to ransack your cupboards for a snack, or something.'

'Yeah, I've seen you when you get hangry. I value my crockery.'

'That was one time, and you caught the plate,' she countered, grinning.

'Still. They weren't cheap. I'll make you a sandwich.' He gave her that same twinkle-in-the-eye look again, and she looked away, half embarrassed and half amused. *Was* Mark Gardner flirting with her?

If he was, she kind of liked it.

TEN

The next Saturday, Ellie found herself back in Mark's kitchen, this time learning how to make Bath buns. The Supremes played on Mark's surround-sound system.

'You know, you have surprising taste in music.' Ellie frowned as she added dry yeast to a pan of warmed milk. 'Aretha Franklin last week, Diana Ross now.'

'You seem to find me surprisin' quite a lot.' Mark shot her a look from the other side of the kitchen island, where he was weighing out raisins. 'What's wrong with Diana Ross?'

'Nothing. I just would have thought, someone like you would like... I dunno... Status Quo, or something,'

'Status Quo?' Mark chortled. 'Thanks.'

'You're welcome.' Ellie giggled. 'Def Leppard, maybe.'

'Bloody 'ell. Kill me now.'

'Soul divas all the way for you, is it?' Ellie peered at the recipe book Mark had propped open in front of her. 'Am I doing this right? I've got to put the dry ingredients in here, then add the butter. Right?' She went over to the gleaming electric mixer and stared at it, trying to work out how to turn it on.

'Yeah. Carry on.' He sat down on one of the high stools at

the steel-topped island and watched her. 'Turn it on at the wall. Then it's the catch on the side to pull up the mixer part.'

'Okay.' Ellie added the ingredients to the bowl, then added the butter before turning the mixer on. 'Oh! It's good, isn't it!' She beamed over at Mark, delighted with herself, as the mix started to form in the bowl.

'Uh-huh.' He grinned back, drinking a beer. They'd had lunch in the garden this time, and the buns were to be an afternoon treat.

Ellie wondered at how she and Mark had fallen into such a pleasant pattern in their time together, without ever having discussed it. Last Saturday, they'd chatted, laughed, baked, drunk coffee and, when their baking was done, they'd eaten it in the garden as the evening approached. Ellie couldn't believe that she'd eaten half a loaf of bread, slathered in butter, with Mark tearing through the other half. They'd also managed to drink a bottle of wine between them as the sun set and the shadows lengthened in the garden.

Mark had asked her back this weekend, and she'd said yes. It still wasn't a date.

They'd agreed, slightly awkwardly, as Mark had said goodbye to her at his front door, that it wasn't a date.

Fee, however, as soon as Ellie had got back to the beach house, had asked her pointedly how her *date* had gone and refused to be persuaded otherwise. She had also pointed out that Ellie had been out all day, and it was ten o'clock before she got home.

The thing was that Ellie had hardly noticed the day passing at all. One moment, she'd been drinking coffee in the garden, and the next, she was shamelessly bloated from eating so much bread, toddling home tipsily across the cool sand of Magpie Cove.

Today, when she'd arrived, Mark had lunch waiting: a fresh mango salad with pan-fried halloumi and a Thai-style dressing which was so good that she'd had seconds. He'd said it was only to make sure she didn't have an attack of the 'hangries' when they were baking, like before, but she knew he'd gone to some trouble in making it.

He must *be seeing someone*, she thought, as the dough mix thickened in the bowl and she slowly added the yeasty milk and some caraway seeds. *No man this good is single.*

'Why are you single?' she asked now, outright, surprising herself.

'Change of topic, but okay.' He raised one eyebrow.

'I'm sorry. I shouldn't have said that. It's none of my business.' Ellie turned off the mixer. 'It says to rest the dough for ten minutes now.'

'Yup.'

'So?' She picked up her beer bottle and took a drink. 'I asked, so you might as well answer.'

'I dunno why I'm single.' He shrugged. 'I just am.'

'Typical man.' Ellie rolled her eyes.

'How?'

'Completely unanalytical. I've never met a man that thinks about why things happen in their love life. You just all seem to... I dunno. Sail through it.'

'What do you want me to say?' He frowned at her and looked away, clearing his throat a few times. 'Haven't met the right person, I s'pose.'

'Do you see a lot of women?' Ellie blurted out. *Am I cross-examining him?* she wondered. She wasn't a barrister, but she knew how it was done in the courtroom. *For goodness' sake, woman, he's not on trial*, she thought. 'I... just don't get it,' she ended, lamely.

'None o' your bloody business!' Fortunately, Mark seemed to find Ellie amusing rather than nosy. 'I dunno. Women want more of a talker. I'm not much in the conversation stakes.'

'We're having a conversation.' Ellie gave him a look. 'Don't play the "hot but dumb" card.'

'You think I'm hot?' He raised an eyebrow, grinning.

Ellie flicked a tea towel at him. 'Oh, shut up.' She was suddenly flustered. 'You know what I mean. Whatever. Forget it.'

Mark laughed for quite a few moments until she flicked him with the towel again.

'I mean it. Forget I said that.' She glared at him, trying not to laugh herself.

'I will forget it immediately. Said what?' He feigned innocence.

'That's more like it. I'm going to look at this dough now.' She turned around, smiling to herself. She was having fun, and she couldn't quite remember ever having this nice a time with a man, basically doing nothing in particular. It was easy being with Mark, like she'd known him a long time and not a couple of weeks. She sneaked a look back at him as he replied to a message on his phone, not watching her, and wondered at what he'd said. She didn't find him quiet at all. *Maybe women in Cornwall are just really picky,* she thought, but it seemed unlikely. It was entirely more likely that Mark had lots of girlfriends and was sparing her feelings.

Ellie returned to her recipe and lifted the dough out of the bowl. Maybe Mark was a gigolo, seeing a new woman every night? Maybe he taught all the women in Magpie Cove to cook in his lovely kitchen, and seduced them with Bath buns in his rosemary-scented garden? Really, it wasn't any business of hers if he did.

But the idea that Mark might be becoming a little more than a friend gave Ellie a feeling of pleasurable anticipation, tinged with a current of fear. She wasn't sure she was in the right place for anything like that yet, but the idea wasn't as unappealing as she might have once thought it was.

'Ready for the next stage?' he asked, looking up from his phone. *Maybe that was another of his women, texting him about a date*, she thought. *But, even if it is, I'm the one that's here now.* And that thought filled her with a surprising warmth.

She smiled. 'Ready.'

ELEVEN

If you had asked her earlier that day if she expected to be back at The Lookout, sipping some chilled white wine with Mark Gardner, it would have been the last thing on Ellie's mind. Yet, here she was, laughing at a joke he'd just made in his quiet, soft-accented voice.

It was the week after their last Saturday baking day and she'd been at the beach house, doing some 'light cleaning' – that was Fee's phrase. Usually when Fee said it, she meant drying up a couple of wine glasses. For Ellie it looked more like pushing the hoover around and putting a wash on: living in a beach house meant that sand got in everything. She had some music on and was wearing some brushed cotton pyjamas with her hair up in a bun when someone had knocked at the door.

'Oh. Morning.' She'd stepped behind the door to try and disguise her unkempt outfit from Mark, who was standing on the step. Madonna carried on singing in the background.

'Mornin'.' He'd given her that slow smile again.

'What's up?' She gave him a bright smile in return.

'I, err... brought you these.' He'd handed her a Tupperware

container containing some lush-looking cherries. 'From the tree, in the garden. Loads of fruit this year,' he explained.

'Oh. Wow, these look amazing. Look, let me just turn this off...' Ellie had scrambled for her phone on the mantelpiece and turned off the music app she was using. 'Classic 80s,' she'd said, by way of explanation. 'No Diana Ross, I'm afraid.'

'Right. Well, no one's perfect.' He leaned against the door frame.

'So, how are the repairs coming?' she'd asked, hoping that her prosthetic boob hadn't slipped out of place as she'd been dancing; she'd been trying to wear it more now that her scar was healing up. Fortunately, her pyjama top was pretty baggy. 'Can't live here forever!' she'd added, jokily, but he frowned.

'Comin' along. Takes a while, though.'

'Oh, no, I know. I was just... never mind.' Ellie had taken a breath. 'Thanks for the cherries. That's so nice of you. I should probably get on,' she'd said.

'You're welcome.' He'd paused. 'Um. I was wondering. If you weren't doing anything later, maybe you'd like to come out for dinner with me? The Lookout does nice food an' that.' He looked like he might be blushing. 'If you haven't got plans. Thought it would be nice if we ate out for a change.'

'Oh! Okay. Shall I ask Fee as well?' Ellie had replied, but his slightly awkward expression had suddenly made her realise that he was asking her out. 'Sorry. Isn't that what you meant?'

'Sure. I can take both of you,' he'd replied hurriedly. 'Walk up to the garage at six and I'll drive us from there.'

When he'd gone, Ellie had gone upstairs to where Fee was working at her laptop on her bed.

'Mark Gardner just asked us to go out for dinner with him tonight.' Ellie had stood in the doorway, feeling confused.

Fee had given her one of her looks. 'Asked you out, more like. I heard all of that.'

'How did you hear? What are you, an owl?'

'Do owls have great hearing? I didn't know,' Fee replied, grinning. 'Anyway, the point is, someone likes you. If you didn't already know from the *Saturday Kitchen* situation.'

'Shut up. He asked both of us. You'd better come with me.'

'Absolutely not! I have no desire to get in the way of love's young dream,' Fee tutted. 'You and I both know he was asking you out on a date. He was just being polite when you assumed it was both of us.'

'Well, I don't want to go on a date with Mark Gardner!' Ellie blushed.

'Shut up. Why are you blushing, then?'

'I'm not blushing,' Ellie retorted. 'Love's young dream? I'm thirty-seven!'

'Love's middle-aged dream, then. Love's thirtysomething dream. Whatever. If he's wearing clean clothes and he's washed his face when you get there, it's a date. What're you going to wear?'

When Ellie had turned up alone at the garage wearing a loose sundress and some summery lipstick, had she imagined a relieved look in Mark's eyes? She didn't know. She'd said that Fee was working that evening and couldn't make it. He'd been very gentlemanly about it, saying that they should all go out another time.

And when they'd got to the pub in Mark's car – something altogether more sleek than his clunky pickup truck – he'd opened the door for her to get out, held it for her as they went into the pub and pulled out her chair at the table.

'So how are your niece and nephew? They're cute kids,' Ellie asked, enjoying the late-evening sun in the pub garden. The sun was getting more and more orange as it moved towards the horizon, and the sea reflected its glow as if it was filled with golden treasure.

Ellie also had to admit that Fee was right: it was clearly a date because Mark was wearing a nice shirt and a clean pair of jeans, and actual shoes rather than his muddy work boots. He'd also shaved and looked like he'd had a haircut. She had tried not to stare, but it was difficult, because Mark Gardner cleaned up very well indeed.

'Ha. They 'ave their moments.' He smiled fondly; Ellie could see the love in his eyes. 'Not bad. My sister's just split up with her fella again, though, so that's gonna be 'ard on them.' He sighed. 'Everyone saw it comin' from a mile away, but Jamey's been tryin' to make it work for years. He's a bad 'un, though.' Mark shook his head.

'A bad 'un?' Ellie probed. 'In what way?'

'Got a temper on him. Slapped her a few times, but not the kids. Last week they had a fallin'-out and he broke her wrist.' Mark paused. 'Sorry. Not really what I wanted to talk about on a...' The word *date* hung in the air between them. '... on a nice evenin',' he corrected himself, clearing his throat.

'That's okay. I'm so sorry to hear that.' Ellie frowned.

'You don't seem very shocked.' He took a sip of his beer. 'Not all us Cornishmen hit women. Or did you think it was common down 'ere?'

'No, of course not! I work in corporate law now, but I started off in family law,' Ellie explained. 'I suppose it doesn't mean I'm very surprised when I hear about it, that's all. I'd probably be more surprised hearing about a happy family.'

'Right, I guess that makes sense.' Mark nodded. 'Not a great headspace to be in, though, is it? Thinkin' that's normal?'

'I suppose not. Anyway, look. If your sister needs any legal help, let me know. I'd be happy to help her out, or point her in the direction of someone else that could help.'

'Oh. Well, I'll pass that on. Thanks.' He drank some of his beer and stared out at the sea for a moment. 'Anyway, I'll be lookin' after the kids a bit more for a while, I expect. Don't mean I won't be doing your repairs, mind,' he added.

'I wasn't thinking about the repairs,' she assured him.

'What were you thinkin', then?' He leaned across the table a little and gazed into her eyes. There was an instant of pleasant anticipation between them: one of those moments in a conversation when the mood changes imperceptibly. Ellie held his gaze for as long as she dared.

'I was thinking that I'm having a nice time,' she answered, honestly. 'And it hasn't been such a great time in my life recently, so thank you.' She looked away. 'I've had a really nice time with you... every time, in fact,' she added, shyly.

'I get that impression. That you're... I dunno. Trying to get past somethin'.' Cautiously, he reached for her hand across the table. 'You can tell me, if you want. But you don't have to.'

Don't tell him, Ellie's mind screamed at her. *He'll just think you're a freak. This is too raw.*

But her instinct, something in her gut, felt that she could trust Mark.

'I had breast cancer.' She said it quietly, not wanting anyone at the nearby tables to hear. 'I had an operation. A mastectomy. That's why Fee and I are here. I'm convalescing.' She gave him a wan smile.

'Oh, God, I had no idea. I'm so sorry.' Mark took both of her hands in his, unexpectedly, and squeezed them. 'How d'you feel now?'

'Tired, still,' she confessed. 'Sore. But it's healing, slowly. It's kind of more about how it feels in here.' She tapped her temple. 'I'm still trying to deal with what's happened. It was all pretty fast. Didn't get a lot of time to process what was happening.'

'You're young to have 'ad it.' He kept her hands in his, gently.

'It can happen. But, yes, I am. Just lucky, I guess.' Ellie

made a face. It was challenging all of her instincts to be this open with someone; she never would be normally, not even with Fee. But there was something about Mark that made her feel like she could. She'd got to know him a little now, and she felt she could trust him.

'Life, huh?' Mark gave her a rueful grin and sat back, letting her hands go. 'Rubbish, sometimes.'

'It certainly is,' Ellie agreed.

'More wine?' he asked, tapping her glass. 'I'll get us another round. Lemonade for me, this time.'

Ellie laughed. 'That seems like a very good idea,' she replied.

On the drive home, Ellie rested her head against the seat and watched the quiet roads of Magpie Cove scroll past, faintly hypnotised by the hum of the local radio station Mark had turned on quietly: it was playing oldies from the 50s, and she recognised the tunes – comforting songs that she could never believe had once been thought radical.

Time changes what we fear, she thought to herself. Once, parents had feared their children listening to rock 'n' roll. Like everyone, Ellie had feared cancer: she still feared it, there was no doubt about that. But she was on the other side of it now. Would it lose its power over her, now that she had had surgery, now that she had had the radiation therapy, now that she was taking the drug that the doctor thought would get rid of whatever was left? She didn't know. It still made her panic when she thought about it too much, so she tried not to. *People aren't afraid that Elvis will corrupt their children anymore*, she told herself. *Maybe, one day, people won't fear cancer anymore.*

She didn't want to think about the cancer, so she pushed it to one side in her mind.

Was she drunk? She'd certainly gone off on a strange

tangent in her thoughts, comparing the music of Elvis Presley to cancer. Mark had drunk one pint of beer; she might have drunk three glasses of wine. They'd both had the seafood risotto, which had been delicious. She wasn't drunk, but since the surgery she'd had a much lower tolerance for alcohol.

She turned her head to watch him as he drove. It was a pleasure to watch him in the dim interior. Ellie studied the line of Mark's jaw, the slight frown on his face as he watched the road; the flex of his muscular forearm as he turned the wheel gently. He cast her a glance, suddenly self-conscious.

'Stop watchin' me,' he murmured.

'I don't want to stop,' she replied, uncharacteristically bold. Not that Ellie was never bold – in her line of work, you had to be. She had to be assertive, even aggressive sometimes. But work was a performance, and she'd never been that confident when it came to men. However, there was something about Mark which made her relax. 'Do you mind?'

'No.' He smiled and looked away.

Ellie hummed along to the next song on the oldies station. She sang under her breath as the moonlit cove opened before her.

Mark stopped the car on the little road that ran alongside the beach. ''Ere we are, then,' he said, a little gruffly. 'I'll walk you to the beach house from 'ere.'

'Oh. I'm fine, you don't have to do that.' Now it was Ellie's turn to feel self-conscious. It was a date: they both knew it was, although they had both pretended that it had just been dinner between new friends. And at the end of a date, people kissed.

Ellie didn't know how she felt about kissing Mark Gardner.

Not specifically Mark. In fact, if she had to kiss anyone, Mark would currently be the top choice unless Henry Cavill suddenly appeared in Magpie Cove, and even then, it would be close. It wasn't about Mark.

It was about her.

'Oh. Okay. Well, then...' Mark leaned over to her seat. Instinctively, she leaned towards him. That was just what you did when someone you liked leaned in to kiss you.

Gently, he reached up and touched her cheek, and leaned in further.

Ellie closed her eyes. It was all right to let Mark kiss her, she told herself. It was all right. She wasn't a leper. She might have one breast, but she was still a woman. She was still a person that deserved affection.

But as she felt his lips brush hers, she pulled away.

'What is it?' Mark murmured, his face still close to hers.

Ellie sat back into her seat. 'I'm sorry. I can't,' she mumbled, grabbing her bag from the footwell of the car and pulling the door handle repeatedly until it swung open violently.

'Ellie!' Mark called as she got out concernedly. 'Are you okay? What did I do?'

Suddenly, she couldn't bear the thought of anyone touching her. Ellie could imagine Mark's face, seeing her naked, which might happen if this continued – not in the car, certainly, but if they started dating. She would be a huge disappointment to him. Not just to Mark – to any man. And she didn't think she could deal with that look on his face, the one that she imagined, on seeing her scar tissue. He would see her and regret asking her out. Regret all the time he had spent with her.

She waved in the direction of the car and strode to the steps to the beach. She heard the car door open and close behind her and willed Mark not to follow her; she already felt mortified.

He called after her again, but she didn't turn around. Ellie broke into a jog as she approached the beach house. There were no footsteps on the sand behind her, and as she stopped at the front door, searching in her bag for her keys, she looked back at the road. Mark was standing by his car with his arms crossed over his chest. Ellie was thankful that he hadn't followed her, but she knew that he wouldn't. She already knew that was who he was.

Finding the keys, she stepped into the beach house and closed the door behind her, feeling a rush of regret tinged with sorrow blossom in her heart.

What had she done? She had ended a perfectly lovely evening by making it uncomfortable. She should never have gone out with Mark in the first place. She had known it was too soon, but she had let Fee talk her into it. And now, whenever she saw Mark – which was going to be often, since he was the one repairing Marilyn – it was going to be awkward between them. And she wouldn't be able to go back to their casual Saturdays: it would feel weird, and she wouldn't want to lead him on.

She'd have to apologise to him. It wasn't his fault. But the thought of seeing Mark again, never mind having to talk about what just happened, made her feel nauseous.

Ellie threw herself onto the sofa and curled up in a ball. She wished, for the thousandth time, that she had never found that lump on her breast. She wished that her life could go back to normal. But she knew it had changed forever, and would never be the same again.

TWELVE

Ellie had been watching the swimmers for a couple of weeks now, holed up in the beach house. She'd told Fee that she wanted some quiet time to rest, which was true, but she was also avoiding Mark Gardner. Fee had given her a knowing look but hadn't pushed it; after all, resting up was what Ellie was supposed to be doing.

The day before, Ellie had been out on the porch, drinking a cup of tea as the swimmers went their various ways up the beach after their swim. A young woman in her 20s, part of the group, had stopped at the house and given her a little wave and they'd got chatting.

Her name was Petra, and it turned out that Petra's old boyfriend had ended up marrying Mara, who owned the beach house. 'No hard feelings. He was too old for me, really. Brian and Mara are, like, made for each other,' Petra had confessed airily. She had told Ellie that she was an artist and used to come to Magpie Cove for the summers as a child. 'Now I live here,' she had explained. 'I've got a really cosy little cottage off the high street. You should come over for tea sometime.'

Ellie had liked Petra immediately. She was a little younger than Ellie, vivacious and warm, with a slightly self-deprecating quality that suggested she knew exactly how pretty and talented she was, but she was confident enough in herself not to show off about it.

It was Petra who had persuaded Ellie to join the group.

'Or, at least, come and dip your toes in the water,' Petra had suggested, leaning on the porch yesterday. 'Come on. We don't bite. It's just five women. Not the scariest of prospects, no? What have you got to lose?'

Ellie hadn't been able to think of a good reply, and so there she was, a day later, with her toes in the water. She did some gentle yoga stretches, feeling her body respond. It was a little creaky, but it all still seemed to work. Ellie was thankful that she'd been so fit before the operation, and hoped her body would still remember how to swim.

Petra was towelling her long red hair dry; she had it in two Pippi Longstocking-esque plaits pinned to her head, but she'd unpinned them and was unpicking the wet links of hair with the towel, rubbing her hair into a kind of resplendent red haze. Ellie thought she looked like a cross between the children's book character and a Pre-Raphaelite queen. She had already been into the sea, but was going back in again now that Ellie had turned up, shyly holding her towel.

'It's only cold for a second. We'll run in. It's the best way, then it's lovely once you're in.' Petra grinned.

It was seven o'clock in the morning, and although the sun was already up – at this time of year, it hardly set at all, with sunset around nine-thirty or ten and sunrise around five a.m. – the sea was still rather cold. Ellie was wearing a baggy T-shirt over a vest and a pair of swim shorts she'd borrowed from Fee, but she still felt exposed.

'Oh, hi, Ellie.' Mara tapped her on the shoulder. 'Great.

You're joining us?' Mara wore an all-in-one shorts wetsuit in black with a red zip.

'It would appear so.' Ellie frowned at the water. 'Petra persuaded me. I couldn't get Fee out of bed, though.'

'She's missing out.' Mara grinned. 'I love the sea at this hour. It's just us and the water. There's something primal about it. Makes me feel closer to my ancestors, somehow.'

Another woman approached the group. She turned to Ellie and stuck out a well-manicured hand. 'Hello! You a new joiner? I'm Simona.'

Ellie shook the woman's hand. 'I'm Ellie. I'm staying at the beach house.'

'Ah, the new tenants. I think I saw you at Lila's party. Welcome.' Simona winked. 'You know, when people come to Magpie Cove, it can be hard for them to leave. You might think you're staying here a few weeks, and it turns out to be forever. Surprised we haven't met properly already, to be honest,'

'Oh. Ha ha. Well, I've been keeping a low profile. And I have a job to go back to, so...' Ellie shrugged. 'Just a holiday.'

'We'll see.' Simona smiled playfully. 'Right. Come on, let's get in!'

Petra linked her arm through Ellie's and they waded into the sea. Ellie tried not to gasp at the cold, but she wasn't entirely successful. She was conscious also that once her T-shirt got wet, it would cling to her, but she was trying not to think about how it would look. She could apparently wear her prosthetic boob in the water, but after much deliberation she'd worn a vest underneath her T-shirt instead of a bra, because she was paranoid the fake boob would somehow fall out underwater.

'What if the sea isn't good for the scar?' she'd asked Fee, but Fee had said that she thought sea water was probably very good for wounds, and she should give the doctor a ring and ask.

Ellie's doctor had confirmed that, actually, swimming was perfect exercise after a mastectomy because it was gentle, and it would help Ellie restrengthen the muscles around her chest and arms. She advised Ellie to start small: twenty minutes of anything but butterfly stroke would be fine, and to take it easy with some stretches before and after.

She walked in, the sea floor mostly sandy with some stones and shells here and there. She'd borrowed Fee's swim shoes too, which had flexible rubber soles and were made of wetsuit material on the top and slipped over her feet like socks.

When they were in up to their waists, Petra held her nose and dunked herself under the water. She came up wet as a seal and gave Ellie a gentle splash.

'Go on. Head under, best way,' she advised, shaking her hair.

Here goes, Ellie thought, and, holding her breath, dunked her head under.

Under the water, everything was completely silent. Ellie opened her eyes. The turquoise water was clear, and Ellie remembered the signs she'd seen around the beach, boasting that Magpie Cove had a special charter or award or some such thing for the cleanliness of its water. She watched Petra's legs as she started to swim away, and turned so that the women were behind her, leaving the emptiness of the water ahead of her.

Ellie started to feel the pressure of the water on her lungs; she couldn't hold her breath for much longer. But before she came up for air, there was a moment when she wondered what would happen if she didn't. Would anyone miss her if she never went back to London? And would anyone miss her if she just never went back – to anything?

The thought frightened her, and she pushed herself up to the surface of the water. Despite everything that had happened to her, Ellie didn't want to die. She didn't want to disappear. She wanted to live. She had had her mastectomy and was taking the drugs that the doctor had given her because she wanted to live. Lying in the hospital bed before her mastectomy, she had vowed to herself, *If I get through this, then I'm never going to waste another second.*

She caught her breath and started to swim, settling into an easy rhythm. Fortunately, her body seemed to remember what to do. She turned to see the other women: two were treading water, talking to each other, but the rest were taking their swims alone, like her. Mara was right: there was something beautiful about being out there so early with just the water and the sun for company.

If you want to live so much, her mind needled her, *then why did you run away from Mark Gardner last week? Kissing him would have been living.*

Ellie turned onto her back to float and rest for a moment. *Because I'm not ready for anyone to... see me, yet,* she thought. *I will be. One day. Just not now. Not a man, anyway.*

Ellie thought of her lawyer friends. The women in the group were always quietly competing about who could be thinner. Ellie had dieted seriously for two weeks before going on holiday on the yacht, even though she already worked out or ran every other day. Now she lay and gazed up at the sun, comparing Petra and Simona and the rest of them to her lawyer friends. She felt pretty sure that none of them would be caught dead in a wetsuit or a baggy T-shirt or any of the floral swimsuits and rubber hats that the other women were wearing to swim in.

Had it always been so easy not to care what one wore? Ellie felt a kind of grief for her past self that had never been allowed – or had never allowed herself – to eat ice creams and chips and float on her back in the Cornish sea, feeling the sun on her face. Even more so, she felt a grief loosening in her heart about never having women friends like these, who didn't seem to care about cellulite and fat, but were in love, and happy, and had friends that liked them enough to get up early and go swimming with them in all weathers.

She wished she had had friends like these women.

And she missed her mum.

Ellie felt a tear escape her eye, and then another. She looked around her, but there was no one nearby to witness her crying. Relieved, she let herself cry. It was a strangely freeing experience. In a way, it felt like the salt water and the sunlight were taking away her sadness – washing it clean on this beautiful summer's day.

One of the most difficult things about having cancer herself was that her mum had had it, and died. Despite her doctor's reassurance that the operation had been very successful, and since Ellie was so young she was more likely to make a full recovery, she was paranoid that she too was going to die. That's what happened to people with cancer, wasn't it? Sooner or later, it got you.

Ellie felt fear roil up in her guts and grip her chest. She started to breathe quickly, and panic took over. What if the cancer came back? What if she died? These were the phantoms that kept her awake at night, staring into the ceiling of her bedroom at the beach house. She hadn't talked to Fee about her fears. She didn't know how.

Ellie started to kick and flail in the water. She tried to slow down her breathing. *It's okay, it's okay,* she told herself, but panic had taken over. She started to imagine that she could see threatening shadows in the water. Were there sharks in Cornwall? She didn't think so, but there might be. She imagined that she felt something brush against her leg. Involuntarily, she screamed. Water rushed into her mouth as she submerged and kicked herself up again. Her chest started to ache.

'Hey. Hey! Ellie. You okay?' Petra had swum over and was treading water next to her. 'It's okay. I've got you.' Petra gently held Ellie's arm, steadying her in the water.

'I'm sorry.' Ellie was crying, mortified, but she somehow couldn't help it. 'I'm so sorry.'

'Stop apologising, silly. Let's get you back on land.' Petra leaned back into the water. 'If you lie back, I can guide you in. Just float on your back.'

'No, I can do it. I can swim,' Ellie insisted. 'I just... I don't know. Got spooked.' She was trying to come back to normal breathing, but fatigue swept her body and mind. 'I panicked.'

'It's okay,' Petra repeated. 'Let's swim back together, then.'

'You don't have to,' Ellie insisted.

Petra gave her a determined look. 'I want to.'

Slowly, Ellie began to do the breaststroke, and she and Petra made their way back carefully to the shore.

'You can put your feet down now,' Petra said, as they were halfway back. 'The sand shelf comes in here. Look, it's safe.' She stood up in the water.

Ellie felt a wash of relief fill her as she felt sand underneath her feet.

'Okay.' She concentrated on putting one foot in front of the other. Soon, she was in the shallows, and walked carefully to where she had left her things.

Feeling weary, Ellie sat on the sand, wrapped in a towel, watching the rest of the women as they took their time in the water. Nobody else seemed to have noticed her panic, or Petra rescuing her.

'You don't have to stay with me. I'm fine.' Ellie looked up at Petra. 'Thanks, though. I don't really know what happened out there.'

'One of those things. Don't worry about it.' Petra drank some water and shaded her eyes from the sun which had now risen and was glinting on the water. 'Anything you want to talk about?'

'Oh. No. I'm fine,' Ellie lied. In fact, her heart was still beating hard in her chest and she felt a little faint, though that may have been to do with not having had any breakfast. But she had only just met this girl, and there was no way that she was going to talk to her about her feelings.

'Well. What d'you think?' A woman, probably in her late fifties, with short silver hair and a friendly face came out of the water to stand next to Ellie, wrapping a lurid beach towel around her thighs and middle and zipping up a hoodie over the top of her faded swimsuit. 'Will you come again?'

'Maybe.' Ellie looked up, shading her eyes. After what had just happened, she wasn't sure. She didn't want to freak out every time she got in the water, but before that had happened, it had been lovely, being in the sea. 'I'm Ellie. Just staying at the beach house for a few weeks while my motorhome gets repaired.' She cleared her throat. 'But it was a lovely experience.'

'Clare.' The woman shook her hand, and returned her gaze to the sparkling sea. 'It is, isn't it? I joined the group about a year ago. I was actually the solicitor that handled Mara's inheritance of the beach house, funny enough. Small world.' She sighed. 'I live up the coast a bit, but I've really got a lot out of it. The swimming group, that is,' she clarified, opening a bag and extracting a Thermos. 'Coffee?'

'That would be great. Thanks.'

Clare rummaged in her bag and brought out another cup, filled it with black coffee and handed it to Ellie.

'No sugar, I'm afraid. I was diagnosed with diabetes a year ago. Hence the swimming. It helps.'

'I'm sorry to hear that.' Ellie took the cup and sipped it; the hot, strong coffee grounded her. She started to feel better.

'Don't be, dear. More common as you get older. I've got a clever little detector thing in my arm, and I can track my blood sugar with an app. An app, of all things!' She clicked her tongue. 'I do miss a glass of wine and I always loved puddings, but it's not that you can't have these things, it's just that you have to be careful.'

'Oh.' Ellie didn't quite know what to say.

'Telling the newbie your war stories, are you, Clare?' Simona appeared at Clare's side, her blonde hair held up with a couple of grips. 'Ellie, we call ourselves the Wild Sisterhood. Because we love wild swimming, yes, but also because in our combined three hundred or so years of being on this earth there's nothing that we haven't seen. You can't shock us.' Simona raised an eyebrow. 'This is a safe space. I want you to know that.' She placed a gentle hand on Ellie's shoulder and sat next to her, on the other side to Clare.

'All right.' Ellie wondered how many of them had actually noticed her little episode in the water earlier.

'No particular reason.' Simona pulled on a jumper and sipped from a bottle of water in her bag. 'Just, I noticed you were a bit protective of your chest. And I wanted to tell you that all of us have something we're a bit protective of. Or something we've been a bit sad about. Me, I've got two C-section scars that mean I'll never have a flat tummy ever again.' She tapped her rounded stomach affectionately. 'That was from the days where they cut you open top to bottom, and then if they had to do it again, they did it the other way. I'm like a hot cross bun if you see me naked, I swear.' She laughed. 'And then, last year, I had a heart attack. Had to have a pacemaker put in.' She rolled her eyes. 'Makes me feel about ninety years old whenever I think about it, but that's life.' She shook her head at Clare and Ellie. 'Anyway, what I'm saying is, whatever you're bringing to the sea, it takes it. The sea accepts us all, whoever we are. And we accept whoever wants to join our little band of warriors.'

'Warriors. You're a hairdresser,' Clare muttered, sipping her coffee.

'*Retired* hairdresser, if you please. So what? I can be a warrior. So can all of us.' Simona gestured at Petra, Mara and another woman that Ellie recognised as the manager of the nice café on the high street. 'All of us step our troubles to the sea, twice a week, at seven a.m. Sometimes I don't want to get out of bed. Geoff always gets hold of me in a bear hug about six o'clock in the morning, and it's quite nice, being there under the covers with him, listening to the cows waking up. And you'll find that some of us here... well, some of us are holding scars you can't see. But all of us come because sometimes we feel heavy with what we have to carry. And all of us step out a little lighter, afterwards.'

Ellie looked around the group, wondering what other troubles these women held – what shadows lived in their hearts. In a strange way, it was comforting to know that she was among other women who had endured difficult times.

'Thank you. For telling me.' Ellie replied. 'I...'

'You don't have to tell us, Ellie,' Mara interjected. 'All Simona's saying is that you're welcome.'

'No, it's all right,' Ellie admitted. 'I have to get used to talking about it.'

Slowly, she peeled off the baggy black T-shirt that she had worn into the sea; the morning air felt good on her skin. She kept her white vest on underneath, but she knew that it was obvious from looking at her, as it was close fitting, what had happened.

'Aw, you poor darlin'.' Simona put an arm around Ellie's shoulders and hugged her, instinctively. 'Bless your heart.'

Ellie started to cry. She didn't mean to, but there was something about the way that Simona, a complete stranger until that morning, had reacted: it was a pure, maternal gesture, and Ellie cried because it had been so long since anyone had enveloped her in their arms in such a protective way.

She had been thinking about her mum, out in the water; and the shock of her own sudden illness and the grief over losing her mum clenched her heart.

'I'm sorry,' she sobbed, trying to compose herself. She was apologising for losing control: sobbing on a complete stranger's shoulder wasn't the done thing, wherever you were in the world, surely.

'Don't you be sorry, my pet. Don't you ever be sorry.' Simona stroked her hair. Ellie was aware of the rest of the women standing around her like sentinels; it was as if she was being guarded.

She heard Fee's voice and looked up, wiping her eyes.

'Ellie! What's happened?' Fee knelt down next to her friend, concern written on her face. 'Are you okay? Did you hurt yourself?'

'I'm okay.' Ellie wiped her eyes and gripped Fee's hand. 'Really. It's all right. I just got upset. It's no one's fault.'

She stood up, and Fee gave her a hug.

'If you're sure. I just came down to see if you guys all wanted to come to the beach house for some breakfast.' Fee looked around the group, still in the dark about what was going on. 'But, maybe another time...'

'No, that sounds perfect.' Ellie sniffed and wiped her eyes. 'I showed them. I had a mastectomy. I had breast cancer.' She said it, bravely, to them all. 'But, before I panicked in the water... that swim was good. So I'd love to come again, if you'll have me.'

'Don't be daft. Course we'll have you.' Petra took her arm. 'And I think I speak for us all when I say I am very up for some breakfast.'

'There's muffins from Maude's Fine Buns.' Fee led them up the beach, towards the house. 'I thought we could sit on the porch.'

Petra glanced up the beach and nodded. 'Perfect timing. Look, there's that group of surfer dudes again. We're just in time to watch them.' She grinned wickedly. 'Just for their technique, obviously.'

'Obviously.' Simona rolled her eyes. 'Honestly, you girls.'

'We aren't girls, Simona,' Petra corrected her. 'We're the Wild Sisterhood, remember?'

'How could I ever forget?' Simona laughed as she climbed the steps to the beach house porch, settled herself in a rocking chair and squinted at the rather toned-looking group of surfers heading for the water. 'Hang on. I need my glasses.' She put them on, and smiled beatifically. 'That'll do nicely.'

THIRTEEN

Ellie was talking to the man behind the counter in the butcher's shop when her phone buzzed.

She was realising that one of the simple pleasures of living in Magpie Cove was doing her grocery shopping every couple of days in the local shops. Some days, she'd bought fresh pollock and herring from the few fishermen left in the cove, who came back with their catch in the early morning. She and Fee were certainly eating like queens, and at least half of Ellie's clothes didn't do up anymore.

She paid for her sausages – delicious, thick pork-and-apple ones that she could imagine would go beautifully with the hasselback potatoes she'd planned to make later, and promised to come back soon.

The thing was, oddly, for someone who had been so obsessed by her weight, that she didn't really care. Fee had never cared anyway, and, as she put it, they were eating healthily, for the most part. They were eating well, and if Ellie had put on a bit of weight, maybe that was because she was returning to the natural weight she should have been at thirty-seven.

'You are *supposed* to have a bum. And hips. And boobs,'

Fee had patiently pointed out to her for the hundredth time as Ellie had tried, and failed, to get her size eight jeans on. 'It's not actually the end of the world to be a size twelve, you know. Or a size eighteen.' She smoothed her dress over her hips. 'Personally, I'd rather enjoy eating, go for some good walks and call it even.'

'I know, I know.' Ellie had sighed, and pulled the skinny jeans off her calves. But quite honestly, Fee was right. There were worse things in life.

Outside the butcher's, she looked at her phone.

Thanks for offering to help Jamey out. This is her number if you want to give her a call still. I know she'd appreciate it.

Mark Gardner had sent her a text, attaching a mobile number underneath, which she assumed belonged to his sister.

Ellie frowned, looking at the message. Three dots flashed underneath it, indicating that Mark was writing another message. She watched them intently, wondering what else he was going to write. She hadn't heard anything from him since running away from him at the end of their date more than a week ago: he had texted Fee a couple of times with updates on the repair, but that was it.

In terms of Marilyn's progress, it was slow. It seemed that although Mark had fixed one problem, there was now something wrong with the gearbox and that, in turn, needed a new part that was difficult to get.

Hope you're well.

The three words seemed minimal compared to the time he had spent composing them. Had he intended to write something else? What, if so?

Ellie stared at the screen, wondering what to write back.

She had no problem in helping Jamey out with some legal advice, but she had no idea what to say to Mark.

Okay, I'll give her a call.

She replied, and then hesitated. What should she say? She knew she'd behaved badly on the date and Mark at least deserved an explanation, but she'd been avoiding it. She already felt like an idiot.

I'm fine. How's things? she added, and regretted it as soon as she had replied. She should call him and speak to him in person and explain why she had freaked out and run away. But then, on the other hand, did she really have to explain herself to anyone?

Repairs going slowly, waiting for the new gearbox, came the reply.

Great, she replied. *How long do you think it will be until she's ready?*

Hard to say, but a couple of weeks, he replied. There was no mention of how he was, or any asking her out on another date. Clearly, Mark had had his fingers burned, and wasn't keen to stick them in the oven again.

It wasn't that Ellie didn't understand – she would have reacted in the same way as Mark, probably, if someone had suddenly got super awkward and run away from her at the end of a date. She wanted to say more. She wanted to explain, but it felt too raw.

Okay, let me know when you have the next bill ready, Ellie replied.

She had been paying Mark every week or so, rather than expecting him to foot the bill for all the new parts Marilyn needed. It wasn't cheap, but Ellie was invested now. If she hadn't had so many savings, she would have had to sell Marilyn early and cut her losses, but now Ellie figured she might as well get Marilyn in tip-top condition. Even if she and Fee didn't have time to take Marilyn for the road trip they'd intended, she could sell Marilyn on as a fully renovated vintage motorhome. God knew that she had nowhere to park her back at her London flat.

She wanted to add something else. She wanted to be having a different conversation: flirty, like that last Saturday in the kitchen when she'd flicked the towel at him. She liked Mark, and she thought that he liked her too.

That was the problem.

Her fingers hovered over the phone. Should she ask him out again?

Will do, Mark replied. There were no more dots indicating that he wanted to add anything else. Ellie's heart sank a little. If there had been a moment to text something more flirty, it had gone.

Ellie walked back to the beach house and called Jamey's number instead. It was a good way to distract herself from whatever was going on with Mark.

'Oh, hi, babes,' Jamey replied when Ellie explained who she was. There was some kind of ruckus going on in the background, and she made Ellie wait while she went and pulled a door closed.

'So, how can I help?' Ellie walked down to the beach and sat on one of the benches looking out over the cove, listening to Jamey's story. Sadly, it was one she'd heard so many times before, but it never got any easier listening to another woman tell her about her abusive partner. Ellie could hear the fear in Jamey's voice as she described what Darren had done. Anger rose within her. *How dare he?*

'All right. I can help you,' she told Jamey, as her legal brain started to fire up again. 'The first thing we need to do is find a good law firm, and I know the perfect person.' She had thought of Clare immediately. She'd have to discuss the case with her, but Clare seemed like one of those solid local professionals you could rely on. Ellie could give Jamey free advice, but she couldn't fight the case for her – her firm would have had to take the case on formally, and she didn't think they would do that. She had checked that Clare's firm could, however – even if Clare couldn't do it herself, being a property specialist.

'I can't afford no private solicitor,' Jamey protested. 'I ain't got that sort of money.'

'Don't worry about that. I'll cover it.' Ellie had already decided that she would pay for what Jamey needed. It was easy enough, and a couple of days of a local lawyer's time arranging a restraining order wouldn't set her back that much. She wanted to do it.

Magpie Cove had shown her nothing but kindness: it felt good to give something back.

FOURTEEN

'Shouldn't be a problem.' Clare was towelling herself off next to Ellie on the beach. Ellie felt amazing after her sun-sparkled morning swim; it was her fourth now, and she was still taking it easy, but she could feel her strength returning. There had been no return of the panic in the water after that first time – but Ellie wasn't taking any chances. She walked into the sea slowly, and if she started to feel panicky, she would stop and breathe in the cool morning air until she felt better. When she was in the water, she floated or did a gentle breaststroke, just for twenty minutes or so. Nothing strenuous, but she could feel her strength and flexibility coming back every time, and she was starting to regain feeling under her arm.

Fee had started joining them now too, and the Wild Sisterhood's breakfast back at the beach house after swimming was becoming a regular thing. No one objected to Fee's provision of coffee and pancakes, bowls of fresh fruit and croissants after an invigorating dip in the ocean. Clare stuck to black coffee, but she liked to come for the gossip.

'Poor Jamey. I've seen her around, here and there. Nice enough girl. Sadly, there's too many nice girls that end up with less than nice men.' She sighed. 'Makes me grateful to be single, I can tell you.'

'I can imagine.' Ellie wrapped a towel around her shoulders. She still wore shorts, a vest and baggy T-shirt to swim, but she was starting to feel slightly less self-conscious about her one-sided flat chest. 'I appreciate it. I can't get involved professionally, but obviously I'll cover your firm's fee. Just tell me what I owe you.'

'Will do. The family judge in St Ives is a good friend of mine. Rowland Hyatt. I'm actually meeting him for dinner tomorrow night, so I'll mention it to him then. And I'll chat to Jamey in the meantime.'

'Rowland Hyatt?' Ellie did a double take. 'Of Hyatt, Rowe and Hoffman?'

'I think so, yes. He was a partner in a London firm and then he moved down here – what, three years ago? Wanted a change of pace.' Clare slid on her sunglasses. 'Why, do you know him?'

'Four years ago. Yes. I did, anyway.'

She had known Rowland Hyatt, once. In fact, he was one of the doomed attempts at a relationship her lawyer friends had tried to engineer for her. Clearly, Rowland had hated going out with Ellie so much that he had run away to the other end of the country a couple of months after they had started casually seeing each other.

'Oh, well then, you should definitely come out with us! I'm sure he'd love to see you,' Clare prattled on, apparently not noticing Ellie's reddened cheeks.

They walked up to the beach house with the rest of the group, went in and sat at the table. Fee busied herself in the kitchen with Mara.

'Oh, I don't know if I should...' Ellie protested. 'I mean, it's been a long time.'

'Nonsense!' Clare cried. 'I'll pick you up at six thirty

tomorrow night. We're going to a nice restaurant in St Ives. Do you good to get out of the village.'

'But...' Ellie tried to protest, but Clare flapped her hand as if to indicate the discussion was over.

'No arguments. Legal eagles' dinner. It'll be fun.'

I'm not sure that it will be, Ellie thought, already wondering what on earth she was supposed to wear out to a 'nice dinner' that didn't show off her mastectomy in a gruesome light. And surely the only thing worse than having to go out for dinner with an old flame was having to go out for dinner with an old flame when you'd just had some pretty unflattering surgery.

Fee placed a plate of American-style pancakes on the table and added a tall bottle of maple syrup. A dish containing some of the Cornish butter that Fee and Ellie had become addicted to sat on the table as well, with a range of non-matching mugs and a jug of filter coffee. Mara was making a pot of tea in the kitchen, and Fee went back to the counter for some bananas and a bowl of strawberries.

'So, we got this through the door.' Fee placed the fruit on the table and helped herself to a banana. She shook the local free newspaper, the *Cornish Star*, in the air. 'Says here that cancer care funding's been cut for all the communities around here. Apparently, you guys used to have a mobile breast screening clinic come down here once a year?'

'Yep. They did cervical screening as well. It was quite handy, really, otherwise you have to schlep all the way to Truro,' Petra replied, taking the newspaper to look for herself.

'Well, it's been cancelled.' Fee smoothed the paper out on the table, next to her plate. 'Budget cuts.'

'Oh, would you credit it?' Simona swore under her breath. 'Honestly. Whoever's making these decisions, they're not women, are they?' She picked up the newspaper and read it. 'What're all the women with no cars supposed to do? The old dears who could just about walk down to the cove to get checked aren't very well going to be able to get to bloody Truro on their own, are they? Truro. I ask you!' She tutted.

'Well, I don't mind driving people up there now and again if needed,' Petra offered.

'Me too,' Mara added. 'But we need a better solution, don't we? I mean, it's all well and good being charitable but we need something more permanent.' She frowned.

'We could fundraise,' Ellie suggested. 'I mean, you can't give the money directly to the council and expect them to replace the cancelled screening service. But a fundraiser could be done for an existing cancer charity. It's something.' She shrugged. 'And in the meantime, we can lobby the council and see if we can get the screening bus reinstated.'

'You can see 'oo the lawyer is round 'ere, can't you?' Esther Christie chuckled. 'Look at you, Ellie. Takin' on the world with two seconds' notice.'

'Well, it's just being sensible,' Ellie muttered. 'Not that Fee and I are going to be here that much longer. But it's worth a go.'

'Oh no, my duck, 'course it is, I was just teasin'. Just like my Connie, you are. You young girls.' Esther patted Ellie on the back of her hand. 'I'll 'elp you, my love. We can do some fundraisin' in the museum if you want.'

'Well, why don't we do a sponsored swim?' Fee helped herself to a couple of pancakes and spread them with a thick layer of soft, golden butter. 'We could make a thing of it. Advertise it like a charity fun run or something. People would love to come and have a summer swim in Magpie Cove: I bet there's loads of people who've never thought to come here. If everyone had to pay £20 to take part, then that'd probably make at least a few hundred pounds for charity. Worth a shot. I can make up some posters, if you want? And advertise on social media.'

'I like the idea.' Petra clapped her hands together. 'And I'm sure we can get some catering going on the beach. We can do it from the café, or Maude at the bakery would love to help, I'm sure. Oliver would help too. He runs a private catering business,' she explained to Ellie.

'Sounds great.' Mara sipped her coffee. 'And let's all write to the council about the breast cancer screening. We could get one of those online petitions going too.'

Ellie was very aware that no one had mentioned her specifically in this conversation: her cancer. Her missing breast. But the implication was there.

'You don't have to do this, just for me. Or because of me,' she said, quietly. 'It happens to so many women. It's not about me.'

'We know.' Simona gave her a level look. 'But it's always about someone, Ellie. That's the point. Cancer affects almost everyone these days, in one way, shape or form. We'd care about this even if you weren't here. But you are. So, we care about you.'

Ellie felt a lump thicken her throat. 'Okay,' she muttered.

Fee stood up and gave her a hug. 'You all right?' she asked, mussing Ellie's wet hair. 'Come on. I thought you were tough. One ladies' breakfast and a fundraising plan and you tear up like a mum at a Christmas carol concert.'

Ellie laughed. 'I am tough. Just, maybe not as immune to kindness as I used to be.' She wiped her eyes.

'Not a bad thing, my love. Life softens us as we gets older.' Esther sighed. 'Still, all the knocks are what makes us human. Eat your pancakes. Put a bit o' weight on them bones.' She pushed Ellie's plate towards her.

Ellie acquiesced. She got the feeling that people didn't often say no to Esther Christie, one of the wise, older women of Magpie Cove. But, also, she didn't want to. It was a relief to have these women in her life: women who were older than her, had been there and done it already and didn't seem to be shocked by anything. The Wild Sisterhood. She'd missed having a strong maternal figure in her life since her mum died, and she appreciated it.

Sometimes, you never knew something was missing until it came along and claimed you.

As she ate her pancakes, Ellie was wondering whether the thing she'd always felt was missing in her life was, in fact, Magpie Cove. She still knew she had to go back to London, but she realised that she'd stopped looking forward to leaving. Part of her never wanted Mark to finish working on Marilyn. Part of her wanted to stay.

Ellie gazed at the women around the table, smiling at their jokes and easy friendship. Would it even be possible to stay here? Ellie had no idea what a life outside London would look like for her, and she couldn't imagine how it would work, but for the first time, she thought seriously about leaving London. What would she really be leaving, apart from her work, which she loved? If it wasn't for that, she couldn't really think of anything she'd miss all that much. And that, in itself, was kind of sad.

FIFTEEN

Ellie was making lunch when she heard a sudden bang from upstairs, followed by the sound of Fee swearing. She ran up the stairs.

'Hey! What happened?' She ran into the study, where Fee was rubbing her foot.

'I'm okay. I was looking for A4 paper in this cupboard and this box fell on my foot,' she muttered. 'Bloody thing. Look at its corners! Who balances a wooden box with razor-sharp edges at the top of a cupboard? Madness.'

Ellie bent down and examined Fee's foot. 'I think it's okay. Can you move your toes?'

'Yes.' Fee waggled them. 'Ouch.'

'I'll get you something from the freezer. Hang on.' Ellie ran downstairs and came back with a bag of peas. 'There you go. How come you were sneaking around in Mara's cupboards, anyway?'

'I wasn't sneaking. I texted her to see if she had any A4 paper in the house, save me heading into town to get some. I don't even know where I'd get any in Magpie Cove. Anyway, she said to look in here.'

Ellie picked up the wooden box. 'I wonder what's in here?' She turned it over in her hands, and looked up at the shelves built inside the cupboard.

'Dunno. Open it.' Fee draped the bag of peas over her foot and sat down on the high-backed chair. 'And let me know if you see any A4 in there. I've got to print out this presentation and post it. Bloody old-school clients. Why I can't just send a PDF, I'll never know.'

'I'm not going to open it. It's Mara's.' Ellie placed it on the desk next to Fee's laptop.

'Well, give it to her, then. She said she was going to pop in this afternoon anyway. Looks like nobody's looked at it for a long time. She might have forgotten it was in there. You don't want to leave personal stuff in rental properties.' Fee reached for a half-drunk cup of tea. 'Ugh. Cold.'

'I'll make you another.' Ellie picked up the mug and the wooden box and took both downstairs. 'Lunch is almost ready, anyway,' she called behind her. 'D'you think you can walk down the stairs?'

'Depends what it is.'

'Sausages and salad,' Ellie replied, smiling.

'Be there in five.'

They were halfway through lunch when Mara knocked at the front door and poked her head in. 'Everyone decent?' she called.

'Come in. We're having lunch,' Ellie replied. 'There's some left, if you want any—?'

'Oh, no. We've just had lunch at the café.' Mara walked in, taking off her black straw sunhat and fanning herself with it. 'Franny's with me. Say hello, Fran.'

Ellie and Fee had met Mara's daughter Franny on a couple of occasions already and liked her immediately: she was a smart, no-nonsense young woman who belonged to a local group of teenage activists who called themselves something different every week, it seemed. Ellie had seen their posters up around the village, usually asking locals to remember to recycle, or vote in the upcoming councillor elections. Ellie thought that Franny would make a very fine local councillor herself when she was old enough.

'Hi.' Franny looked up briefly from her phone.

'D'you want some sausages, Franny? From the butcher in the village.' Fee pointed to the large bowl on the table.

'No, thanks. Meat is murder,' Franny replied, then added, 'Thanks, though,' after Mara gave her a look.

'Principles don't take up room from manners,' Mara lectured her daughter, who rolled her eyes.

'Okay, okay.'

'Sorry about her. She's never very chatty when she's in the middle of organising an online petition,' Mara explained. 'I brought you some paper, by the way, Fee. We had some at home. And I brought you some more toilet paper and dish-washer tablets. Noticed it was all running a bit low.'

'Oh, thanks, Mara. You're a lifesaver.' Fee took the stack of A4 paper, wiping her hands on a tea towel first. 'Oh, and we found something of yours up in the study. I knocked it off the top shelf by mistake, but we thought if it's personal you should have it at your house, really.'

'Oh! Thank you.' Mara took the box, frowning. 'I've actually never seen this before. Where did you find it again?'

'There's a storage cupboard in the study. At the top,' Fee repeated. 'Fell on my foot, actually.'

'Is your foot okay?' Mara leaned over to look at it.

'I'm fine. I've iced it.'

'Well, I don't know what this could be. I thought we'd got all of the personal items from the house when we started renting it out,' Mara mused.

'Just open it, Ma,' Franny called from the sofa, where she

had her feet up and was tapping away furiously at her phone. 'End the suspense.'

'Okay, okay.' Mara smiled and unfastened a little brass lock that looked like it had once held a key: fortunately, it didn't seem to be locked.

The box, a dark varnished wood that looked as though it could be either hundreds of years old or twenty, was inscribed with ornate initials on the top.

'IVH.' Mara looked thoughtful. 'The "H" would stand for Hughes, if it's Mum's family. The "I" might by Ivy. I think that was my grandmother's name. I don't know if she had a middle name beginning with "V", but it's entirely possible.'

'How can you not know your grandparents' names?' Franny called out. 'Ancestry.com, Ma.'

'I know they were called Ivy and William, but I don't know much about Mum's family at all. She never let me see them,' Mara replied. 'A few people around the village have told me things. My grandfather was quite an influential person here, once. But the scandal around my mum having a baby out of wedlock, as a teenager – that was really difficult for them. That I do know.'

Mara opened the box. Curious, Franny put her phone down and came to stand next to her mother.

'What is it?' she asked, tracing her fingers over the inscribed initials. 'What's inside?'

'Letters, I think.' Mara brought out a few envelopes, foxed with age. 'A locket. Look, Fran. It opens.' She placed the oval locket on a silver chain in her daughter's hand. The front was an ornate silver frame around a black jewel, and when it opened, a faded photograph was inside.

'Who's that?' Franny held it up to the light. Mara narrowed her eyes at it. 'I don't know, darling. But she looks like you, don't you think?'

'It might be her. Ivy.' Franny stared intensely at the photo.

'There's definitely a likeness.' Ellie looked at Franny's dark hair, plaited and pinned to her head, her high cheekbones and wide eyes, and then back at the photograph. 'When would this have been taken?'

'I don't know exactly. My mum was born in the 60s so I guess her mother would have been born in the 40s, maybe? Whoever it is looks young in this. Maybe the late 40s, early 50s, if it is her?'

'What else's in there?' Franny reached into the box. 'What's this?' She pulled out an ornate black card and read it aloud.

William "Billy" Hughes
Grieve not for me, my life is past
I dearly loved you to the last;
Grieve not for me but pity take
On my poor children for my sake.
Farewell, dear wife, my life is past
May you and I unite at last.
Mourn not for me, nor sorrow take
But love each other for my sake.
Death did to me short warning give
Therefore be careful how you live
Prepare in time, make no delay
For I was quickly called away
"Not my will, but Thine be done."

'Nice poem.' Mara took the card. 'This was made for my grandfather's funeral, then. I wonder if Mum went. She never told me.' Mara turned it over in her hands. 'No date on it.'

'Maybe you should take this all home and look at it there?' Ellie suggested, seeing that this was becoming more and more emotional for Mara. 'I'm sure your son would like to see it too.'

'Yes.' Mara wiped her eyes quickly and flashed a bright

smile. 'That's a good idea. Come on, Fran. Let's let Fee and Ellie get on with their day. We'll catch up with you soon, guys.'

'Okay.' Ellie could see that Franny was fascinated with the box, but Mara was walking a difficult line between wanting to see what else there was, and not wanting to see, either. She could understand that. Mara was someone who had rebuilt her life in Magpie Cove; she had found Brian, and they were happy. Whatever was in the box, it could tell her about her past. But some things were better left unknown.

Ellie knew that memories could hurt. Sometimes she wished she could put her grief at losing her mum in a box and lock it away somewhere in her heart, out of harm's way. Instead, she had lost herself in her work, over the years. If she worked hard enough, she could fall into bed at the end of the day so exhausted that she didn't have to think about her mum at all.

But, here, with more time on her hands than she'd had for twenty years, she'd found her thoughts coming back to her mum. Her intense bravery, fighting the cancer she too had found – first, in her breast and then later, all over her body.

Ellie shivered, though it was a hot day. She saw Mara and Franny out, and grabbed her sunglasses from the table.

'I'm heading out for a walk,' she called over to Fee. 'I'll be back later.'

'You okay?' Fee asked, surprised, but Ellie shook her head.

'I'm fine. Just need to get out.'

'All right. Take some sunscreen, then. You'll burn otherwise.' Fee tossed her a tube of sun protection, a concerned look on her face. 'You sure you're okay?'

'I'm fine.' Ellie waved in Fee's general direction and walked onto the beach.

It was better outdoors. It was a Wednesday, and the beach was relatively deserted: just a few surfers milled at the water's edge. Ellie started walking around the sandy perimeter of the beach, rubbing sunscreen onto her arms and chest, and doing as best as she could with her back, hoping that she wouldn't come home with a hand mark on her back like she had the last time she'd applied her own sun cream.

Though it was late lunchtime and the sun was high in the sky, the breeze off the sea made it feel more hospitable than the close heat inside. Ellie wondered how Fee could work in it, but she had two fans up in the office which kept it relatively cool.

Since she'd been in Magpie Cove, Ellie had avoided thinking much about her mum's cancer and her own, but she knew she couldn't avoid thinking about it anymore. If the wild swimming and the fresh air had been helping her to heal, then it was also breaking down the barriers she had painstakingly built up to avoid thinking about the things in her past that she didn't know how to handle.

Her mum had got breast cancer when Ellie was just fifteen. She had been forty-five. It was no age at all, Ellie thought – just eight years older than she was now. That, in itself, made her take in a deep breath and let it out slowly. She was actually younger than her mum to have had it. Despite her healthy-living regime. Despite her dawn runs along the river Thames.

Like Ellie, her mum had had a mastectomy. She had minimised the impact as best she could for Ellie, to the point of telling her not to bother coming into the hospital to visit. Ellie had been sent to stay with her dad, who was still living nearby, before he moved abroad.

Obviously, Ellie had insisted on being by her mum's bedside every available moment. In fact, the nurses had had to tell her to go home. She'd prayed to a God she had never really believed in to save her mother: *Please, please, let her be okay.* She had bargained with the powers that be, offering her teenage life in exchange. *Please, save her*, she had repeated, thousands of times, in her mind, under her breath, whispered to the beeping of the heart-rate monitor and the rough, clean white sheets that covered her mother as she slept.

If there was a God, it had not taken her life in return for her mother's, but Ellie's mother had nonetheless gone into remission and that was blessing enough. She'd stayed that way until Ellie had started university three years later. But that time, no amount of tears and prayers had been able to make the cancer submit to mercy.

Is that my fate? Ellie thought as she walked up the beach and onto the road that led out of the village. *Should I be planning for a shorter life than I expected? How long do I have?*

She started climbing the steep path that led to Magpie Point, the cliffs that overlooked the cove to the right of the beach. She'd been up there a couple of times, but so far it had always been an effort to get there. Today, she noticed that she was stronger than she had been before, and though she still got out of breath, it wasn't as bad as before. *I am healing*, she thought. *I have to focus on that.*

When she reached the top of Magpie Point, Ellie sat at the edge of the cliffs and stared out to sea, catching her breath. Her arm had better movement than it had, and the feeling was definitely coming back. She moved it in gentle circles, rotating her shoulder.

What had happened to her mum was sad. But even though she had had cancer, too, at such a young age, it didn't mean that she would end up in the same boat. She knew that. But it was one thing to know something in your mind, and another thing to know it in your heart.

She was scared of what might lie ahead, and she felt the weight of her mum's legacy like a weight around her neck.

SIXTEEN

'Ellie McTavish, look at you!' Rowland Hyatt stood up as Ellie and Clare walked into the laid-back seafood restaurant Clare had been raving about for the whole drive over. As Ellie had thought, Clare really hadn't taken no for an answer about coming out to dinner and had come to knock for her at the beach house.

Ellie had been busy all day and had, in fact, only just returned to the cottage in time from the council headquarters in St Ives. The local buses ran on 'Cornish time' to some extent, Ellie had learned, which meant that they turned up more or less when they felt like it. Earlier that day, she'd been waiting for an hour at the bus stop, and then the driver had taken his time down the winding roads back to Magpie Cove, stopping at several small villages and helping pensioners and mums with buggies on and off. Still, it was nicer than the London buses where no one ever talked to anyone else, she supposed.

At the council, Ellie had spoken to a local councillor about getting the screening bus reinstated, without much luck. The woman was apologetic, but explained that with budget cuts, there were many services that had to go. It wasn't ideal, but their hands were tied.

'However,' the councillor had said, 'if the people of Magpie Cove wanted to run their own bus to the clinic in Truro, they are free to do so. In fact, I've heard that Magpie Cove now runs its own community café. Clearly, people there are enterprising. They'll sort something out.'

Great. Thanks, Ellie had thought, sarcastically. *Nothing like relying on local do-gooders to fill in the holes the state has left empty.* The councillor was right: people in Magpie Cove did look out for each other. But what about other villages that didn't have the same number of 'enterprising people'? Was it fair to leave them without vital services? How would they cope?

Despite the tortoise-like bus journey home, Ellie was ready for dinner when Clare knocked. Ellie wore a pretty, loose white blouse and dark-dyed blue jeans. She carried some black high heels over the sand of the cove, and put them on in Clare's car, taking care to dust off the sand from the soles of her feet before she got in. Fee had persuaded her to pack them before they'd set off from Ellie's apartment, back in London. 'You never know,' Fee had admonished her. 'I believe they do actually have wine bars in Cornwall.'

And so, here I am, having dinner with my ex fling, Ellie thought to herself as she painted a smile on her face which she hoped didn't look too forced. *You really couldn't make this stuff up.* She was still cross from the council meeting, but she'd worry about that later.

Rowland and Ellie's relationship had been very short-lived. It had been three dates and one attendance at a dinner party as a sort-of couple before they had broken it off, and Rowland had left for Cornwall shortly after that. At the time, she'd been relieved. Rowland leaving had put a definite end to Ellie enduring any *maybe you'll get back together* conversations with her female friends in the group. At the time, she'd been so relieved to be out of the gossip mill that she hadn't really kept in touch with him after he left.

Now that Ellie saw him again, she remembered how good-looking he was. Rowland was that kind of old-school, tall, dark and handsome guy in his late thirties who always wore well-cut suits, held the door open for ladies and had perfect manners. However, once you got to know him, the veneer revealed a wicked sense of humour and a talent for witty conversation. Ellie had been entertained by Rowland, although sometimes he made jokes at other people's expense that could be a little cruel.

One of Ellie's dates with Rowland had been a day out at Ascot. Ellie wasn't a big fan of the famous horse race, having been before. It started out well, and you were expected to dress up, which was nice – Ellie always appreciated an opportunity to wear something that wasn't work wear. But everyone drank so much. The champagne flowed nonstop, and as the day wore on, everyone got drunker, ruder and louder. Ellie, even though she had had a few drinks herself, had not greatly appreciated being in the midst of a band of braying toffs who roared at the horses, but more frequently at each other and the bar staff. At least Rowland had apologised to the waitress on behalf of their friend who, having drunk quite a few glasses of champagne, had snapped at her for bringing him the wrong vintage bottle.

At the end of the day, as they got into a taxi, another of their friends had cheerfully confessed that he'd lost several thousand pounds gambling. Apparently, he hadn't been bothered by the loss, but Ellie had been appalled. Her mother would have been able to buy a car with what the guy had just thrown away on nothing. They had never had a car, in fact, Ellie and her mum. It was another of those things that most people took for granted that Ellie had grown up without.

'Rowland Hyatt.' Ellie kissed him on the cheek. 'Good to see you.'

'Wow. What's it been, four years?' He held out Clare and

Ellie's chairs for them to sit, and then sat down himself, smiling from ear to ear. 'You look great, Ellie.'

Clare cleared her throat pointedly.

'Oh. Clare, you always look amazing, you know that,' Rowland added quickly, grinning. 'What a coincidence, though. You bringing Ellie McTavish to dinner. Here on holiday, Ellie?'

'Yes. Well, kind of. My friend Fee and I came to Cornwall on a road trip, then got stranded in Magpie Cove temporarily.'

'Magpie Cove's gain, if you ask me,' Clare added. 'I'm hoping she'll stay.'

'I wholeheartedly agree. You must stay. Cornwall's got some top-notch restaurants now, and some of the properties are breathtaking, if you stay away from the deprived inland towns.' Rowland's eyes twinkled. 'This calls for champagne!' he gestured to the waitress, then turned back to the table.

'So how long did you two go out together?' Clare took a bread stick from a glass on the table and crunched it.

'Oh, just a few dates,' Ellie replied, quickly. 'It was very casual, then Rowland moved here.'

'Remember the picnic?' Rowland raised one eyebrow. 'I planned a beautiful date at the Rose Garden in Regent's Park. Packed a picnic from Fortnum's. Beautiful sunny day. Ellie arrived looking like a fairy-tale princess. She was wearing this kind of gauzy, floaty pink dress. D'you remember, Ellie? We drank champagne sitting among the most glorious roses. I kissed you for the first time there.'

'I do remember.' It had been a beautiful, perfect day, she had to admit. And Rowland had been so sweet, asking her permission for a kiss, and reading poetry to her among the roses.

'She's my one that got away.' Rowland gave Ellie a misty look. 'I really did some soul searching before I left London, I can tell you. But the job offer was too good to turn down, and anyway,' he gave Ellie a playful look, 'Ellie never seemed to have much time for a relationship. She was always working. I didn't think I'd ever be able to compete.'

'That's not fair. You were just the same. You came down here to be a district judge, for goodness' sake,' Ellie protested. 'Not exactly something you can phone in.'

'Maybe. Anyway, the job came up and I'd been looking to get out of corporate legal. Plus, I've got family here, so I thought it was too good an opportunity to miss.' Rowland gave Ellie an unreadable stare. 'But I would have considered staying if I'd thought there was anything to stay for. If you'd have given me a chance.'

Ellie took a champagne glass from the waitress who'd brought drinks, and let her pour it. What was she supposed to say to that? She had no idea that Rowland had liked her that much. He'd left without much fanfare, although he had sent her a very heartfelt email after leaving that she hadn't known how to answer, and so didn't.

'I didn't know that,' she confessed. 'But I guess it just wasn't the right time.'

'I guess not.' Rowland met her gaze, and they shared a quiet moment, neither one of them looking away. Ellie was remembering how sweet Rowland could be, and she'd forgotten how attractive he was too.

'If you two want some time on your own, say the word,' Clare interjected. 'Only, I'm really hungry, and I've planned for this dinner blood sugar-wise. So, I'll just eat quietly.'

Rowland laughed loudly. 'Not a bit of it! I am not a man to renege on dinner plans with a lady. It's just not every day you get to reconnect with Ellie McTavish.' He looked down at his menu, and blinked a few times. 'Oysters, I think. Shall I order for us all?'

Ellie adored oysters, and she'd heard that they were a speciality of this restaurant.

'That sounds perfect.' She drank some of her champagne.

Almost instantly, she started to feel lightheaded and giggly; this was what hardly drinking and recovering from an operation did, she supposed.

Unexpectedly, this was turning out to be a very pleasant evening.

'So, Rowland. A little shop talk before the food arrives.' Clare sipped at her glass, and outlined Jamey's case briefly. 'We'll be submitting the paperwork shortly, but I just wanted to let you know it was coming, and if you think there'll be a problem getting the restraining order. Of course, it will have to go through the family court, too, in terms of access to the children.'

'Shouldn't be a problem. Bloody shame what some women have to go through, mind you. It wasn't until I came to Cornwall and started working as a judge that I realised how many cases like this come through. You don't see it in corporate legal.'

'Do you miss the corporate side?' Ellie was curious. 'I mean, everything's so... slow, down here. Not much going on, work wise.' She'd been continuing to think about her own work situation.

'You'd be surprised. More work than we can handle coming through the family courts, and the criminal.' Rowland shook his head. 'I don't miss corporate law in the slightest. Helping out real people with real problems is much more satisfying. And I get to go to the beach any day I want.'

'Where do you live? Here?' Ellie had to admit that St Ives was a gorgeous place. She and Clare had walked past Michelin-starred restaurants, posh bars and all kinds of boutique shops on the way from the car to the restaurant.

'Just up on the hill. Great view of the bay.' Rowland sipped his champagne. 'You'll have to come up and see it. Come for dinner.'

The waitress arrived with a huge platter of oysters placed

on ice and sprinkled with lemon zest and chilli flakes. She set it on the table carefully, and wished them *bon appétit*.

'Wow. I think my stomach just leaped into my mouth.' Clare reached for an oyster, smiling contentedly. 'In a good way.'

'That would be lovely. I'd love to come for dinner.' Ellie actually meant it. She was enjoying seeing Rowland again, and she realised she hadn't thought about her mastectomy at all until that moment.

'Also, if you were interested in a job down here, we're always on the lookout for good people. You wouldn't be bored.' He raised an eyebrow. 'Think about it.'

'I will.' Ellie met his eyes again. Was it possible that there was something still between them? Rowland was now a judge, had moved to the seaside and seemed generally more relaxed than he ever had in the past. And Ellie didn't have to worry about impressing her social group anymore, or about them being nosy about her and Rowland's relationship, because they weren't there. Everything was different now.

'To old friends, and new beginnings.' Rowland held up his glass for a toast.

'Old friends.' Ellie clinked her glass on his. 'And oysters, of course.'

SEVENTEEN

'You know, that'll stop ringing when you answer it.' Lila Bridges eyed Ellie's phone, which was buzzing on the table next to her in Serafina's Café.

'It's work. I'm ignoring it,' Ellie explained, and switched off the ringer altogether. The phone screen lit up after a moment with a voicemail message.

In fact, Ellie had volunteered to contact some local newspapers to let them know about the wild swimming event that her group was planning at the end of the summer. Ellie would be back at work by then, but she had promised to come back for the weekend.

If she was being really honest, Ellie didn't know if she'd have the energy to return to Magpie Cove for a weekend, but she didn't want to disappoint everyone. The cancer fundraiser was because of her, after all.

She had been trying to compose an email on her phone that made the sponsored swim sound interesting and fun, and it wasn't coming easily to her. If it had been a legal brief, she would have found it much simpler.

'I see.' Lila held a coffee pot in one hand. 'Refill?'

'Lovely, thank you.' Ellie held out her blue pottery mug. 'They want me to go back. I mean, I'm supposed to go back. I've put them off for another week, but there's only so long I can do that.'

'And you don't want to go back?'

'Not sure.' Ellie looked out of the window onto Magpie Cove's small high street. 'I mean, this was – is – just a holiday. I've had holidays before and never had a problem going back to work. But I guess I've never had breast cancer before. The whole thing's just knocked me for six, if I'm honest.'

'Of course it has. I'd be amazed if it hadn't.' Lila sat on a spare chair at Ellie's table; the café was pretty quiet. 'You seem to like it here. You've got roses in your cheeks,' she added.

'I do like Magpie Cove. That's the thing. After everything that's happened, I don't know if I can face going back to that life again. I don't think my body can take it anymore. And... I dunno. Maybe it was a sign that I shouldn't.'

Lila sighed. 'Only you can make that decision, sweetheart. All I can tell you is that I came down from London to study patisserie in St Ives, and I never looked back. I fell in love with Nathan, but I also fell in love with the cove. There's something special about it.'

'You lived in London?' Ellie sipped her coffee.

'Worked in a dead-end job. Hated it. My boyfriend and I split up after I had a miscarriage.' Lila frowned. 'I can talk about it now, but I was a wreck when I got here. But I just needed to get away, and I found this course I wanted to do, and hey presto. It all came from there. Nathan left a job in the city, too. He much prefers it out here.'

Ellie had met Nathan, Lila's partner, in passing a couple of times. He was rather shy, but Lila said he warmed up when you got to know him. Lila and Nathan owned the café: Serafina's had been his mother's before she died.

'Well, that's because he met you here, I expect.' Ellie smiled at her new friend. It was strange, but Magpie Cove already felt like home.

'Partly. He had some bad feelings about the village when he got here, but it's changed a lot. I dunno. People seem to come here and it... heals them, somehow.'

'Sounds a bit new-agey.' Ellie raised her eyebrows.

'I know. But it does. I think, sometimes, people need community around them, and that's what you get here. And a simpler life. And the sun and the sea swimming don't hurt you, either.' Lila gave Ellie a meaningful look. 'And neither will the local talent.' She lowered her voice as Mark Gardner pushed the glass door to the café open, setting off the tinkling bells.

Lila stood up. 'Hi, Mark. Baked potatoes on the menu today.' She winked at Ellie and followed Mark to the counter.

Why is she winking at me? Ellie wondered. *It's not as if I have a thing going with Mark Gardner.* She busied herself with her phone, but looked up as he approached her table.

'All right, Ellie?' Ellie was still getting used to the soft Cornish burr of the local accent, and the way that people said 'all right' instead of 'hi' or 'hello'. There were a lot of other strange Cornish-isms that she was starting to pick up, too, mostly from Esther Christie in her swimming group. Esther was of that older generation that had grown up with all the strange Cornish legends like piskies in the tin mines, smugglers and local fairies.

'Hi, Mark.'

'Wanted to say thanks again for helping Jamey. She says that lawyer's been really good.'

'You're welcome.' Ellie smiled up at him.

'Can I sit down?' Mark looked awkward.

Ellie looked at all the other empty tables in the café. 'Umm. Okay.' She felt self-conscious, suddenly realising that she hadn't bothered putting any make-up on that morning, and her hair was in a messy topknot. She was dressed comfortably in jogging bottoms and a T-shirt. *He must think I'm the worst-dressed woman in the world,* she thought to herself. Still, she didn't have to dress up for him, she reminded herself. 'I, um... I actually had dinner with the judge the other day. Turns out he's an old boyfriend.' Ellie gave a little laugh. 'So I know the case is in good hands.'

'Old boyfriend?' Mark frowned, but just then Lila deposited a plate with a giant baked potato topped with cheese and baked beans, complete with a huge salad, in front of Mark, and a glass of water. Ellie assumed it must be Mark's usual lunch.

'Oh. Yes. Well, not really a boyfriend as such. We just dated a little bit a few years ago. Small world.' Ellie's stomach grumbled as she glanced at Mark's baked potato, which looked like it could be an advert for baked potatoes everywhere: huge, crispy and piping hot, with a mound of topping and a rivulet of butter running down the side. 'So, how's Marilyn getting on?'

'Pretty good. Should have her up and running in about a week.' Mark shovelled his lunch into his mouth; Ellie reflected that the sight was a world away from the sophisticated champagne-and-oyster dinner she had enjoyed with Rowland. Even if Mark was naturally gorgeous, no one looked appealing if they ate like a pig. She averted her eyes politely.

'You must be looking forward to getting back to London?' He posed it as a question, and Ellie wasn't sure how to answer.

'Oh, right. Yes.' She didn't feel like discussing it again, and not with Mark, who she wasn't sure how to be around. There was always a slightly awkward vibe between them, not made easier by the fact that whenever Ellie saw Mark, she felt a little bit breathless. She couldn't quite explain it, but if she had to describe the feeling, it was a pleasant nervousness. She hadn't felt like that with any other man, including Rowland: with him, conversation came easily as they had so much in common, but with none of the strange butterfly tummy. She didn't know which was better or worse.

She certainly had very little in common with Mark. *If I watch him eat, it might make me fancy him less,* she considered, and made herself watch him wipe his mouth with the back of his hand. Sadly, it had no effect, other than bringing her attention to his mouth.

'Right.' He looked back down at his plate.

'Sorry that we—'

'I guess that—'

They had started talking at the same time.

'Sorry. You go.'

'No, no. After you.' He looked embarrassed. There was an uncomfortable silence.

Ellie didn't know what she'd been about to say, but if it was something about their disastrous date, then the moment had passed. She cleared her throat.

'I really appreciate all your hard work on Marilyn,' she said, instead. 'I mean, I guess I'll have to sell her when I get back to London, but she'll fetch a better price by being actually roadworthy now, so that's good.'

'You're going to sell her?' Mark actually looked upset. 'Really?'

'Yeah. I mean, I've got nowhere to keep her. My flat has one allocated parking space for a normal-size car, not a huge motorhome,' Ellie explained.

'Oh. Right.' Mark focused his attention on his lunch, eating mechanically. Ellie could sense that he wasn't happy about something.

'What?' she asked, directly.

He looked surprised.

'What d'you mean? I'm eating my lunch,' he replied, a little mutinously.

'You're upset about something. Because I'm going to sell Marilyn?' She frowned.

'None of my business.' He shrugged. 'Just a bit of a shame, that's all.'

'Why? It was just your job to repair her,' Ellie argued.

'Right. Just doing my job.' Mark forked another bit of salad into his mouth. God, why was he being so monosyllabic? Ellie wondered why he'd bothered to come and sit by her at all.

'Don't worry, I'll pay you everything I owe you.' She watched him, unsure what was going on.

'Well, that's all right, then.' His voice had a sarcastic tone. He shovelled the last of the potato into his mouth and stood up. 'I'd better get back to work.'

Before she could say anything, Mark had taken his plate back to the counter.

What the hell is going on with him? Ellie stared at his back as he paid Lila at the till, and gave her the briefest of nods before leaving the café. Had she hurt his feelings in some way? What had she said? That she was selling Marilyn, that she was probably going back to London soon? Why had he even sat down at her table in the first place?

Save me from these impossible, monosyllabic men, she thought. She couldn't imagine Rowland being this way. In fact, you'd have a hard time making him be quiet.

As if he knew she was thinking about him, Ellie's phone flashed up a text from Rowland inviting her to dinner at his house that evening.

Hi there, Ellie That Got Away, dinner at mine, 7 p.m.? Tagliatelle is on the menu. Will text the address.

She smiled, and tapped out:

Sure, sounds good. I'll bring wine.

Rowland replied immediately with his address and the wine glass emoji.

It would be nice to spend an evening with him, catching up, Ellie thought. Someone who understood who she was, and the life she'd had. Perhaps it was fate that had brought them both to Cornwall. Perhaps this was a sign. She wasn't sure what it might be a sign of, but the prospect of seeing Rowland felt good, anyway.

EIGHTEEN

Rowland's house was as lovely as Ellie had expected.

As the taxi rolled slowly up the gravel drive, after being buzzed through the tall wooden gates that swung open when the driver approached, Ellie gazed up at the large manor house that revealed itself behind a riot of pink and blue hydrangeas. Sitting in lovely wraparound gardens, Rowland's home looked as if it was straight out of a magazine. The Georgian façade was painted white, and a porch guarded the wide, wooden front door, which Ellie realised featured a cast-iron door knocker in the shape of a squirrel when she stepped up to knock it.

'Ah, Ms McTavish, welcome, welcome!' Rowland opened the door with a flourish almost as soon as she had knocked, holding a champagne glass in one hand. 'Come with me, and we'll get one of these for you,' he added. 'I'll take your jacket.'

Rowland opened a door off the long hallway, putting his drink down on a delicate side table nearby, and hung up Ellie's jacket on a hanger on a coat rack.

'Thanks. Rowland, this place is amazing!' Ellie looked around at the high ceilings, the Georgian mouldings and the parquet tiled floor.

'I'm glad you like it. I bought it as a bit of a tip, actually, then did it up slowly, when time allowed. Had some help here and there, of course. I never claimed to be a handyman. Still, it's surprising what you can do when you learn. If you'd told me when I lived in Kensington that I'd learn how to wallpaper a room, I wouldn't have believed you.'

'Well, it's lovely,' she repeated.

'I'll give you the tour later, if you want. Anyway, come and get a drink for now. Dinner's on.'

Ellie followed Rowland along a long hall and through to a beautiful kitchen, where he crouched before a vast marble-topped island and extracted a chilled bottle of champagne from one of two wine fridges built into it. He poured Ellie a champagne flute and handed it to her, placing a kiss on her cheek as he did so.

'To you,' he said, clinking her glass with his.

Ellie was a little taken aback by the kiss, not that it was anything other than Rowland being sociable. But, still, the caution that she felt now about anything related to her body, or about being intimate with someone, acted like a leaden coat around her. Her instinct was to avoid all physical contact, all risk of her mastectomy being discovered.

But you don't have to pull away from a friendly kiss, Ellie reminded herself. And it was true that, since she'd joined the swimming group, she had slowly started to feel more positive about her body.

It was seeing other women's bodies that had helped. Specifically, the bodies of the women she swam with, who were anywhere from their late twenties to their late sixties, and were gloriously imperfect. She had started to realise that if she thought Simona, Esther, Petra, Mara and Clare were beautiful – and they all were, in their own way – then it was possible that she, also, could have a body that was worthy of love – if only from herself.

Baby steps, she'd told herself as she'd got ready to come to Rowland's house. *Not like you need to enter* America's Next Top Model: *at this stage, you need to be able to look at yourself without flinching when you get out of the shower.* And she had begun to do that, recognising that one scar wasn't the totality of her appearance or existence.

There was still a way to go, but at least when she'd had a shower for the past few days, and she had stopped and really looked at herself in the mirror, she had not hated what she'd seen. That felt like progress.

'So what's for dinner? You said pasta, I think?' Ellie walked over to an impressively shiny silver range stove.

'Tagliatelle with king prawns, chilli and lemon. Followed by chocolate pots.'

'That sounds delicious. Could you always cook and I just never knew?' Ellie looked around for evidence of cooking, but the surfaces were impeccably clean.

'Full disclosure: I can't cook. But I have a wonderful local caterer.' Rowland put a silver stopper in the neck of the champagne bottle and replaced it in the fridge. 'Imagine what would have happened if I could cook? You would have proposed years ago, probably.'

'Maybe.' Ellie laughed. She couldn't help thinking about Mark, and the fact that he could turn out a mango salad as well as all manner of baked treats, as well as knowing how to change a carburettor.

'Goodness. You don't need to find that quite such a hilarious prospect.'

'You moved away!' Ellie protested. 'I didn't have a chance to get to know you better. Or for you to learn to cook.'

'Come on. I think we both know that's bullshit.' Rowland upended his glass, finishing it. 'I really liked you, but you were a closed book. You were well known for it. I could never work out how to melt the ice queen.' He shrugged.

'What?!' Ellie perched on one of the high stools that sat around the kitchen island. *Ice queen?* 'What do you mean? Well known for what?'

'You never talked about your past. You never expressed a preference for anything. You always agreed with' – Rowland waved his hand vaguely – 'your friends, you know. I've forgotten their names now – Pinky and Perky.'

'Toni and Suzanne,' Ellie corrected him. 'That is not true!'

'Oh, it is. You just always went with the flow. That's nice and everything, but it didn't make it very easy to know you. I'd ask you what you wanted to do on the weekend, and you'd always say you didn't mind. And then when I chose where to go, I'd get the distinct impression you weren't really having a good time. Remember Ascot? You hated that.'

'Yes, I did. But only because everyone got screamingly drunk. And you all threw away so much money that day. It was offensive.' Ellie shot back.

'Right. See, there's the woman I was trying to get to know. Why didn't you say so at the time – that we were being offensive bastards? Why did you even come, if you hated horse racing so much?'

'I didn't hate horse racing. I hated everything that went with it. The drinking, the rudeness. The excess. The money you all gambled that day could have bought my mum a car. Or paid her gas bill for a year.' Ellie sighed.

Rowland laid out two plates on the table and leaned down to a glass-fronted fridge, taking out a white container and dumping it into a pan on the stove.

'Look, I get it. We acted terribly. I look back on those days with embarrassment, believe me.' He shook his head. 'We weren't living in the real world then. But what I'm saying is, why wouldn't you ever say what you were thinking? And why didn't you ever talk about yourself? I mean, I know Toni told us that your mum had died. I think that was before I knew you. But otherwise, it was... *pffft.* A blank slate.'

Ellie thought for a minute before she responded, trying to decide how she could best explain what being inside a bubble of privilege was like when you came from a very different background.

'I didn't know that you thought that about me. That anyone thought that, in fact. All I was trying to do was fit in.'

'You did fit in.'

'No, I didn't,' Ellie explained, patiently. 'You don't know what it's like, growing up poor. I got a full scholarship to Oxford. I had loans up to my eyes. Yes, because of who I knew at Oxford and the fact that I did well there, I got a good job and I paid off my debts. And I lived the high life with you and everyone else. I won't pretend I didn't enjoy it, because I did, some of the time.'

'I seem to remember you enjoying it as much as anyone.' Rowland turned on the heat under the pan and frowned at it.

'But a lot of the time I could just feel my outsider-ness around me all the time. You lot would exchange stories about your childhood, about your nannies and au pairs and learning to ski when you were five, and prep school. I didn't have any of that. I grew up just with my mum in a really poor town, and it was only because I happened to be brainy and I worked my ass off that I got out of it. So I didn't talk about my past, or about my life outside the bubble, because I had nothing in common with all of you,' Ellie finished.

'I see.' Rowland stirred the pan and then took it to the table, dishing up tagliatelle onto the plates he had put there. 'Dinner's ready, if you are.'

'I am.' She sat down, feeling oddly empowered by her rant.

'I didn't know any of that.' Rowland went back to the wine fridge and brought back a bottle of white wine and two chilled wine glasses. It was a warm night, and the wide bifold doors were open. Beyond, Ellie could see a concrete patio with some expensive-looking garden furniture placed on it. There were no plants at all, but there was a nice view of the sea. Again, Ellie couldn't help comparing Mark's green garden full of fruit trees with this concrete lounge area. It seemed sad not to have a garden in Cornwall.

'Well, it's true.' Ellie twisted her fork in the tagliatelle and ate some: it was tasty though rather lukewarm.

'Anything else I don't know? Any other secrets bubbling away in that beautiful head of yours?' Rowland poured them both a large glass of wine.

Ellie took hers, thinking she was going to have to pace herself if she was to avoid getting drunk and being put in a taxi by eight o'clock.

'Well, yes, actually. It's not a secret, but' – she took a breath – 'the reason I took time off work and came down to Cornwall was that I had breast cancer, and I had a mastectomy.'

She took a sip of her wine, despite her warnings to herself. Every time she said it, it got easier, but it was never by any means easy, and she doubted it ever would be.

'Goodness. Wow, I'm so sorry. Ellie, I had no idea.' Rowland put down his wine glass and stared at her. 'You're okay now?'

'I'm fine. Recovering. I've been swimming in the sea a lot.'

'That's good. Not just the physical scars, though, is it? Very emotional thing.'

'It is.' Ellie met Rowland's gaze, a little surprised.

'What?'

'Nothing. I just don't remember you being this... mature.' She chuckled a little.

'People learn and grow, Ellie. My goodness.' He raised an eyebrow at her and started to eat. 'I'm sorry that happened to you, though. Cancer's a bastard.'

'It is indeed.' Ellie speared a fat prawn with her fork. 'But, I dunno. I was going to say something corny like it's given me a chance to change my life. You know what I mean, I suppose.' She gestured to the house.

'I know all about big changes,' Rowland agreed. 'And I know that I've learned more about you in the past half hour than I did for the three years we hung out at parties and on holidays, and definitely for the handful of times we dated.'

Ellie shrugged. 'It's all ancient history now, anyway.'

'It doesn't have to be.' Rowland was watching her with an uncharacteristically serious expression.

'What does that mean?'

'What it sounds like. I always liked you, and I'd like to start getting to know you again now. Properly. Date. Whatever,' he continued.

'You want us to date?' Ellie frowned at him.

'Maybe. Why not? This is nice.'

'It is, but...' Ellie ate some more pasta to give herself time to think. 'This is all coming out of the blue a bit, Rowland. Can't we just have dinner without complicating anything?'

'Sure. But that's where I am in this, just so you know.' He took another drink. 'I understand if you need some time to think about it. But I'm putting my cards on the table. Most un-lawyer-like.'

'Well, you are a judge these days,' Ellie replied, smiling. 'Look, it's very sweet of you to say all of this. But I'm not really ready to date right now. What with the operation and everything.'

'All right.' Rowland shook his head. 'I understand.'

'You're not too devastated, are you?' Ellie teased him a little, but she was grateful. The worst thing would have been finding herself in a man's house, alone with him, and him deciding to make a move on her and not taking no for an answer.

'I *am* completely devastated, but I live in hope.' Rowland's eyes twinkled. 'Do you want to talk about it? The cancer? I mean, I don't know what to say about it really, but we can.'

'Not really.' Ellie felt her defences go up. She did not want to talk about it, and if that made her an ice queen, then so be it. 'But thank you. One day, maybe. For now, I'd really love you to take my mind off it. Tell me some of your stories. You always told really hilarious stories.'

'Challenge accepted.' Rowland laughed. 'Now, where to begin...'

Later, when they'd finished the chocolate pots and the bottle of wine, they wandered outside. Ellie looked down at the other houses she could see from their vantage point: many had pools, and surprisingly few of them had the verdant gardens she would have expected.

'You have some view,' she said.

'I do,' Rowland agreed. 'You'd be amazed what you can see people doing from up here.'

It hadn't been what she'd meant, but she didn't correct him.

Ellie shivered; it was still warm, but there was a cooler breeze coming up from the sea. 'Oh. How ungentlemanly of me. Here, take this.' Rowland picked up a blanket that was draped over a sun lounger and placed it gently around her shoulders.

As his arms circled her, Ellie looked up into Rowland's soft brown eyes, and something passed between them. It wasn't the electric feeling she had felt when Mark Gardner had tried to kiss her – before her panic had set in, and she had pushed him away. She didn't feel awkward around Rowland, and she wasn't sure if that was a good or bad thing. Rowland was a known quantity.

But it was a nice feeling, a sense of knowing him. And there was something nice in knowing that Rowland liked her – wanted her, even – despite what had happened to her.

Gently, Rowland lowered his head and kissed her: briefly, and then more deeply.

Perhaps it was the wine, or perhaps it was the fact that Rowland had told her that he still had feelings for her, and that gave Ellie the upper hand in the dynamic between them. Or maybe it was that she already knew Rowland: he'd been a friend once.

Whatever it was, when Rowland kissed her, Ellie didn't pull away, and she didn't immediately worry about her breast or her scar or the idea that Rowland might find her physically repellent in some way. Instead, she kissed him back.

It felt good. It was nice. Comfortable.

Instinctively, Ellie wrapped her arms around Rowland's neck; his hands travelled to her waist, and he pulled her gently towards him.

'Oh, Ellie.' Rowland breathed in her ear. 'I should never have left you. I should have...' He trailed off, and kissed her again.

Ellie was the one that stepped back, touching his cheek affectionately as their embrace separated.

'Don't,' she murmured.

'I'm sorry. Was that too much? I don't want to... you know. Make you uncomfortable,' Rowland murmured.

'It wasn't too much. It was good,' she replied.

'Okay.'

'Okay.'

The shadows on the patio were growing, and the golden light was dimming.

'Ellie?'

'Yes?' Ellie looked up at Rowland. She felt strangely at peace. It was just a kiss, but it was a milestone for her. She could kiss a man. She had done it, and Rowland hadn't run for the hills just yet.

One day, maybe, she could do more.

'Do you want to come inside for coffee? And I mean that in a completely literal and non-suggestive way.'

Ellie laughed.

'That would be lovely, Rowland,' she said, and followed him back into the bright kitchen.

NINETEEN

Ellie was sitting on one of the rocking chairs on the beach house porch, trying unsuccessfully to read a novel. It was a hot day and the sea was calling her, but because it was mid-afternoon, the beach was busier than when she went wild swimming in the mornings, and she was shy about going into the sea in front of strangers.

Fee had gone to Exeter for the day, a few hours' drive away, borrowing Petra's car for the journey. Apparently, she'd been doing some graphic design for the university there and they'd been so impressed with her work that they wanted to talk to her about a possible lecturing job.

Ellie found herself watching the people on the beach: a few surfers, people with dogs, a few old couples and mums with little ones, paddling at the sea edge. Ellie was thinking about how life just carried on, despite everything: the sun rose and set every day, whether you had had cancer or not. Toddlers paddled, dogs barked and old ladies wore cardigans on the beach even on a baking hot day. There was something reassuring about the way that the world carried on even when it felt like it had stopped for you.

She was also thinking about what Rowland had said, the other night. He had called her an ice queen. She'd never thought about herself in that way before. Was she so remote and inaccessible?

She picked up her phone and ran off a quick text to Toni before she could decide against it.

Sorry if I've been a bit distant. I just find it really hard to talk about what's happened. Hope you're having a good day. It would be really nice to talk if you have time. I miss you xx

She didn't think she'd ever signed off a text to Toni or any of her friends with kisses before, or sent a message that felt so raw and honest. But it felt good to have done so. Even if Toni never answered, Ellie would know that she had, at least, tried to be more open.

Shading her eyes with her hand, she watched as two children ran onto the beach, followed by a young woman in pink shorts and a white vest. Ellie realised that she recognised the woman: Jamey, Mark Gardner's sister. She slid on her sunglasses and picked up her book.

It wasn't that she didn't want to say hello, but Ellie thought that she didn't want to make Jamey feel uncomfortable by seeing her, and knowing that Ellie knew about what was going on in her personal life. If Jamey came over to say hello, then Ellie would talk to her, but she wasn't about to go over there and intrude.

Still, Ellie watched from behind her book as Jamey ran after Amber and Danny, splashing them and making them squeal when she got to the clear, turquoise water. The kids waded out farther, the water up to the edges of their shorts. Ellie could hear Jamey laughing, calling out to them, perhaps warning them not to get their clothes too wet. Jamey waded out closer to them and caught Danny in a bear hug. It was lovely to watch them, and Ellie felt a sudden pang of something she didn't quite recognise in herself. She'd never wanted kids, never been much of a kid person at all, but as she watched the easy way Jamey hugged and played with her children, Ellie felt a sudden yearning.

A text flashed up on her phone. She reached for it, thinking it would be Toni's reply, but Rowland's name sat at the top of her notifications.

Great first date the other night, Ellie. Let's do it again soon, my beautiful Ice Queen.

She looked at the text for a moment, thinking how to reply. For anyone else, the text would be a bit forward, but Rowland was just that kind of big personality from whom you expected grand gestures and big talk. In a way, she'd always found him a little hard to read, because he was like that with everyone, from the postman to waitresses and people he'd just met.

Before she could think of anything to text back, a shout rang out across the beach, and Ellie looked up at the sound of a man's voice. She squinted against the sunlight.

'Oi! Danny! Amber!' the man yelled again. He was striding purposefully down the beach towards Jamey and the children. Ellie sat up in her chair. The man's whole manner – the tone of his voice, the shouting and what Ellie could see of his expression – put her on the alert.

In the sea, splashing with the children, Ellie could see that Jamey hadn't heard him. He strode down the beach, and as he got closer to the beach house, Ellie could see that his face was set in a grimace.

'Jamey! Oi!' the man shouted out again, and this time Jamey heard him and turned around. Some other people on the beach had noticed, too.

'Darren, you're not supposed to be here!' Jamey yelled back, and Ellie noticed that she stepped forward so that the children were behind her.

'What the hell's this?' Darren waved a piece of paper at Jamey, following up his question with some swear words that made Ellie flinch.

So, this was Jamey's abusive ex, and Danny and Amber's father. And, Ellie assumed, the piece of paper in his hand was presumably the legal paperwork for Jamey. She got up and started walking down to the water line, grabbing her phone from the table as she did so.

Ellie approached the man carefully. 'Hey, Darren. Can you just calm down? This isn't nice for the kids to see.' She really wasn't in love with the idea of confronting an angry man who had a history of hitting women, but she wasn't about to just sit there and watch him terrorise Jamey and the kids.

'Who the hell are you? Sod off. I'm talking to her,' he said, pointing at Jamey.

'Well, you're not talking, actually. You're shouting and swearing, and there are kids here,' Ellie explained in a conversational tone. 'And unless I'm mistaken, I think you're under a temporary restraining order, and there's going to be a full court hearing. So, I'll have to call the police. What you're doing constitutes a violation of the restraining order, which can lead to fines, the permanent removal of your visitation rights from your children, or a custodial sentence.' She held up her phone, realising that it was about to run out of charge. She angled the screen away from him so that he didn't see, and hoped that Darren didn't force her to make the call, because she'd look pretty stupid talking to no one at the end of the line. Still, Ellie held her ground and met Darren's ferocious stare.

'What the... how the hell do you know about that?' Darren's brow furrowed. 'What are you, like, a detective or something? Sod off. I told you, I want to talk to Jamey.'

'She doesn't want to talk to you,' Ellie replied. 'Go away. I'm calling the police. I'm dialling 999.' She tapped the numbers into her phone. 'I'm serious.'

'Darren, leave it!' Jamey shouted. Amber had started crying, and Jamey held her daughter in a tight hug. The sea water had soaked both children's shorts by now, and the sun went behind a lone bank of cloud. The afternoon had suddenly taken an unexpected turn, and the atmosphere on the beach had darkened.

Darren stepped forward and, taking Ellie by surprise, he knocked her phone out of her hands. It landed on the wet sand just in front of the incoming tide. 'I warned you to stay out of it!' he snarled.

Ellie stooped as quickly as she could to pick the phone up. As she did so, Darren strode into the water after Jamey and the kids.

'Help!' Ellie shouted, knowing that she wouldn't be strong enough to pull Darren away from Jamey, and not wanting to get into a fight with him, or worse. She waved at the other people on the beach. 'Help, please!'

Two of the surfers along the beach dropped their boards on the sand and ran over, but before they could get to Ellie, someone else sprinted past her and into the water after Darren, tackling him spectacularly.

Darren made a surprised *ooof* noise as the other man's body slammed into his, and there was a huge splash as both of them hit the water. Both were soaked immediately. Darren sat up in the shallow water, gasping, and pushed against the other man.

'What the—?' Darren coughed, swearing.

Standing up, soaked through in shorts and a white T-shirt, Mark Gardner grabbed Darren's shirt by the collar and wrenched him out of the water.

'Let me go!' Darren shouted, twisting, but Mark held him firmly.

'Get out of here. You've been told. You're not supposed to come within half a mile of Jamey and the kids,' Mark growled.

'Sod off. They're my kids.'

'You gave up your right to be their dad when you hit my sister.' Mark shoved Darren hard in the direction of the beach. 'Move. I'm callin' the police now. And if you wanna try knockin' my phone out of *my* hand, have a go. See where it gets you.' Mark shoved Darren again as he pulled his phone out of his pocket and dialled the police.

Ellie thought his phone must be unusable as it had been dunked in the water along with the rest of him, but he started speaking into it so she guessed it must be all right.

'Police, please. I'd like to report an assault.'

'Fine, I'm going,' Darren shouted. He waded out of the sea, past Ellie. She stepped aside, not wanting to get close to him again. 'Bitch,' he muttered, as he passed her.

Ellie felt a wave of fury knowing that, as grateful as she was to Mark for showing up just at the right time, Darren had only stopped what he was doing because another man had forcibly stopped him. Even the fact that she had threatened to call the police hadn't been enough.

Mark came to stand next to her, talking on the phone. Jamey and the children were wading out of the water too.

'Hey. You okay?' He tapped the phone to end the call and touched her arm gently. Mark shook his head; his blond hair dripped with sea water. The fury in his eyes had been replaced with concern.

'I'm fine. He just... it was just upsetting, that's all. My phone's okay. Look after Jamey and the kids.'

He held out his arms for the children who ran to him, both now crying. Mark enveloped them in a big bear hug, squatting down in the shallow tide. Ellie could hear him talking to them quietly as she reached out to Jamey and held her hands. It was a little awkward, but she did it nonetheless.

'Jamey. Are you all right? I'm so sorry... I saw him, and I tried to intervene,' Ellie explained. Jamey was shaking, and it wasn't with cold: Ellie knew what shock looked like when she saw it. 'It's all right. Look, he's gone.'

They watched Darren retreating up the steps at the far edge of the beach. Even from that far away, Ellie could see the fury in his posture.

She was still on high alert herself, but at the same time, as she watched him go, Ellie thought about why she'd started working in law in the first place. Why she'd wanted to study it at university at all, apart from the fact that it was a good job and paid well.

It was never the money that attracted Ellie, really, although she'd ended up running with that crowd. It was justice that had appealed to her then, and she realised that justice still meant so much to her now. The law wasn't perfect by any stretch of the imagination, but at least it was one way to help people who needed it, and it was something that could, at least in theory, protect the vulnerable.

Real justice might never visit Darren, whatever that justice might be. Ellie could imagine some pretty suitable punishments for him as she stood there, watching him go.

She doubted that Darren would ever know the desperate fear Jamey must have felt protecting her children from him. Ellie knew that mothers felt guilty at any time their children suffered. She knew that all mothers felt that deep protective urge for their children: that they would automatically stand in front of a speeding train to protect them, or any other threat. Jamey had put her body between Darren and the kids without even thinking about it.

And Ellie had always felt passionate about protecting others – women, children, and anyone poor or impoverished or suffering at the hands of a powerful few – in the same way. But she had forgotten that, somewhere in the world of corporate law, takeovers and mergers. She'd been offered a job in corporate law, and after losing her mum – and growing up without any of the things her friends thought of as essentials – she had grasped the opportunity, fearing another one wouldn't come. The salary was large, and it got larger as she wrapped it around her like a security blanket.

Ellie had never stopped caring about women and about justice, but for a long time she'd been distracted by the security her job gave her. It filled the lack that had always been there in her life: the never having enough she had felt so keenly as a child.

But although her bills were paid and she had a nice flat and some expensive dresses, Ellie still wasn't happy.

'What if he does it again? I thought that restraining order was supposed to stop this happening.' Jamey's teeth were chattering. 'I can't rely on Mark to turn up every time. It was just lucky he was supposed to be meeting us on the beach this afternoon.'

'I'm going to get the kids ice creams.' Mark came and hugged his sister. 'You okay?'

'I'm all right. He never got to me.' Jamey wiped her eyes, smudging her mascara. She forced a smile for the kids, and Ellie's heart broke for her even more, watching her pull herself together for the children. 'Hey, that'll be nice, won't it? It's okay. Daddy's gone now. He was just a bit angry.'

They watched Mark start to walk up the beach holding hands with Amber and Danny. He was still wet through.

As soon as the children had turned away to walk with Mark, Jamey started crying, her body slumping.

'Come in and have a cup of tea.' Ellie squeezed Jamey's hand. Jamey nodded, and let herself be led to the beach house. 'It's all right now.' Ellie soothed Jamey as best she could, letting the younger woman lean on her as they walked.

As Jamey made her way up the steps of the beach house, Ellie glanced back at the beach. Mark Gardner was normally so quiet, and yet he'd acted like some kind of avenging angel just then. She took in his back, the wet T-shirt clinging to his prominent muscles, his strong legs in the wet shorts, and his unruly blond hair, a shade darker than usual because of the sea water. The two children holding his hands seemed even smaller because of his strength. She was glad he had been there.

As if he could feel her sudden glance, Mark looked back at the beach house. Ellie blushed and looked away instantly, as if she had been caught doing something she wasn't supposed to. Yes, she was glad he'd been there, but it was more than that. He'd been so... heroic, just now. Strong.

She berated herself for looking away. It was to be expected that she might glance up to check the children were all right. There might be a million reasons why she would have gazed up the beach in Mark's direction, especially given what had just happened. She should have waved, or something. To be friendly.

As she followed Jamey into the beach house, Ellie looked back over her shoulder, and Mark was still looking at her. His gaze seemed to do something electric to her.

This time, she waved, and he gave her a brief wave back.

'Let's get the kettle on.' Ellie closed the door behind her, striding into the kitchen as Jamey sank onto the sofa. She was prattling away to put Jamey at her ease, but all she was thinking was how weird it was that she had spent a whole evening chatting easily to Rowland – and even kissed him – and couldn't even wave at Mark without it becoming awkward.

Perhaps there's a reason for that, Ellie's mind whispered, but she ignored it. She had got good at ignoring her instincts over the years, and it was going to take some practice to start listening to them. For now, it was time to focus on Jamey, and for that she was grateful in an odd way. There were only so many emotions she could deal with in one go.

TWENTY

'Ellie! You found us okay, then?' Simona Gordon cried as she opened the heavy farmhouse door, enveloping Ellie in a hug. 'Come in, come in.' She ushered Ellie into a wide hallway with a long coat rack and a selection of muddy wellington boots arranged in a not-so-neat row underneath. On the other side of the hall, an oak cabinet supported a messy pile of letters and paperwork and a collection of cacti. A wide stairway with wooden treads, all slightly bowed in the middle, led upstairs. Fee was working on a job that had to be done by the next day; Ellie had promised to fill her in with all the gossip.

'This is a lovely house,' Ellie remarked as they walked through into a huge, rustic-styled kitchen with cream-painted wood cabinets and a terracotta tiled floor. The rest of the wild swimming group were sitting at a long, dark wood kitchen table, where Ellie spotted a couple of bottles of rosé wine, one of which was already empty, and the other half full. 'Hi, everyone,' she said, waving.

'You're so sweet, thank you. Mind you, you might think differently if I hadn't moved all the washing off the table before you got here, and cleaned up after the dogs. Honestly, this house is a tip most of the time.'

'Pull up a chair, Ellie!' Petra called out. 'The Wild Sisterhood is now in session!'

'Have you been here long, Simona?' Ellie hung her handbag on the back of the chair next to Petra and sat down. 'Living in the house, I mean.'

'Oh, gosh. Generations.' Simona went to the fridge and extracted another bottle of wine. 'My husband's family, that is, the Gordons. I grew up in the village too, but closer to the cove. I went to school with Geoff, my husband. Kismet, it was. We got married when I was eighteen and I moved in up here. Mind you, his parents still ran the farm then. We spent years living out of one room until they retired and we took over.' Simona sat down at the table and poured Ellie a large glass of rosé.

'It's a dairy farm, isn't it?' Ellie took the glass and sipped it. 'Cheers, everyone,' she added.

'Cheers!' Everyone raised their wine glasses in a toast.

'Best dairy farm in the south-west,' Simona replied, proudly.

'Where are Geoff and the boys tonight, then?' Clare asked. 'Are they hiding from us rowdy women?'

'They're at the pub.' Simona rolled her eyes. 'The Lookout. It's Geoff's second home, since Alex opened it. That's my son. The middle one,' she added, for Ellie's benefit. 'Tim, my oldest, runs the farm with Geoff now. Our youngest graduates from university soon, so he'll be back home no doubt, making more washing.'

'Oh, the pub up on the cliff at Morven? I've been there,' Ellie said, remembering her date with Mark Gardner. She cleared her throat. 'Must be nice, having your own pub,' she added, to move the conversation on.

'Ah, well, there were some teething troubles at first. But yes. He's happy, and it seems to be going well. Got a young lady in his life now too.' She grinned over the table at Esther. 'Esther's daughter, Connie. Engaged. We're waiting for a wedding date. She's keeping Alex on his toes, I can tell you.'

'Christie women don't suffer fools gladly,' Esther exclaimed. 'Not that Alex is a fool in anyone's book. Lovely fella, he is. You got a young man, Ellie?'

'Me? Oh, no,' Ellie said, feeling suddenly under the spotlight as everyone at the table turned to look at her.

'I saw you at The Lookout with Mark Gardner. Couple of weeks ago.' Simona leaned over and prodded Ellie's arm. 'What was that all about? Looked like a date to me.'

'Oooh, Mark Gardner!' Petra cooed. 'So handsome. He used to go out with my friend, Emma.'

'It was not a date!' Ellie exclaimed. 'He's just repairing my motorhome,' she said, playing with her wine glass.

'That's what they all say.' Petra raised an eyebrow. 'Don't you think he's good-looking?'

'I suppose so,' Ellie admitted. 'Please can we stop talking about it?'

'Hmm. Did he ask you out?' Petra wheedled. 'Come on. You can tell us.'

'Yes, but that doesn't mean anything.'

'Oh, it does!' Petra clapped her hands together. 'He's famously shy. If you get more than three words out of him, then he's making a huge effort.'

'Well, we did... do... have quite a good chat when we see each other, I suppose,' Ellie admitted. 'But that doesn't mean anything,' she repeated.

'You've been on more than one date?' Petra whooped. 'Girl!'

'Sounds like Mark opened up to you,' Mara interjected. 'He must like you.'

'He does not,' Ellie repeated. 'He was just being... I don't know. Hospitable.'

Esther tapped her fingers on the table. 'Mark my words, my love. I've known Mark Gardner since 'ee was a boy. Always been quiet. Had 'is 'eart broken a fair few times too. I don't wonder it's because 'ee's not much of a talker. You modern girls all want these long conversations, I dunno what. But time was when a girl'd be grateful for a nice, loyal man with 'is own business. An' if 'ee's a man o' few words, the ones 'ee does say are all the more important.'

'That's a good point,' Simona agreed. 'Geoff can be quiet, but he says the things that matter. And anyway, actions speak louder than words. If you know what I mean, ladies?' She winked. Everyone laughed.

'Oh, leave Ellie alone, you busybodies.' Mara giggled. 'Ellie, ignore them. If there's nothing going on between you and Mark, then I believe you.'

'Thanks.' Ellie knew that she was blushing. She took a sip of wine to cover her embarrassment.

'I'm sure you'll keep us posted if there are any developments—?' Petra said, her eyebrow raised.

'Of course.'

Ellie's phone lit up. It was another text from Rowland.

'Oooh, is that him now?' Petra picked up Ellie's phone.

'No, it's... just a friend. Well. An ex-boyfriend.' Ellie took her phone back and looked at the text from Rowland.

'Looks like your ex wants you to go out with him Wednesday night.' Petra shimmied in her chair. 'Aren't you the dark horse!'

'Well, I don't know if I will,' Ellie desperately wanted the conversation to end and the focus to move away from her. 'It's complicated.'

'Come on, Petra. Leave the poor girl alone.' Clare made a face at Ellie, who shot a grateful look back. 'Let's check in with the fundraiser organisation, and then we can concentrate on the important bit: wine.'

'I've been sorting the food stalls. I've got six so far, nice range of things. Ice cream, traditional Cornish stuff, some vegan options, curry, noodles. That kind of thing. I've checked their insurance and permits,' Mara said.

'I've got the permit paperwork in for the event itself with the council,' Clare added. 'Shouldn't be a problem.'

'Awesome. Well done!' Petra high-fived Clare. 'I've created an Instagram account and been posting about the event. Mara helped me with making some logos and images. We're doing well for followers, and I've been in contact with some of the local tourist organisations. Ellen at the Shipwreck and Smuggling Museum's been handing out flyers I made, and I've put them in the café and in all the shops.'

'Mara? How've you got on with the T-shirts?' Simona put on her glasses and peered at her watch. 'Oh, Lord – I forgot I had a pizza in the oven. Carry on without me for a minute.' She flapped her hands at all of them and got up, picking up a pair of oven gloves as she went. Ellie watched as she approached a cream-coloured Aga, flicked open one of its cast-iron doors and deftly extracted the pizza.

'Okay. I've got a few different options.' Mara held up three different T-shirts. 'This one, I'm not sure about.'

The white T-shirt Mara held up was emblazoned with the slogan 'I GOT WET AT THE MAGPIE COVE WILD SWIM 2022' in bold black letters.

'Well, I like it. But I'm not sure it's the message we want to send.' Clare snorted.

'What's wrong with it, my love? You *do* get wet in the sea.' Esther looked mystified. Petra patted her arm fondly. 'I know, Esther. But it has a bit of a double meaning.'

'What double meaning?' Esther looked around the table. 'What is it? Why are you all gigglin'?'

'I'll tell you later.' Petra cleared her throat. 'Mara, what else have you got?'

'Okay. There's this one.' Mara held up a blue T-shirt with a picture of a sandy cove and a bright blue sea in a circle, with the words 'MAGPIE COVE WILD SWIM 2022' around it. 'It's nice, but it's the most expensive option. If we still charged £20 a ticket, we'd make twenty per cent less for fundraising, after costs.'

'Hmmm. What's the third one?' Clare took a crisp from an earthenware bowl in the middle of the table. 'Don't let me have more than ten of these, by the way.'

'I CONQUERED THE COVE. MAGPIE COVE WILD SWIM 2022.' Mara read the third one aloud. 'This is my favourite.'

'I like that one too.' Ellie nodded.

'Me too. I vote for that one,' Petra agreed.

'And me. If we really think we can't have the first one,' Clare added. 'Esther? Simona?'

'Looks good to me, my love.' Esther smiled. Simona waved from the kitchen.

'Whatever you ladies think,' she called out. 'I've got some garlic bread coming out in a minute.'

'Ellie, how'd you get on with the newspapers?' Clare asked.

'Oh. Okay, I think. I've had emails back from the *Cornish Star* and the *Express*.' Ellie looked at her phone. 'They offered to write up an interview with one of us the week before the event. I've also got advertising rates for both, if we want to do that.'

'You should do the interview,' Clare said. 'Tell them about why you came to Cornwall. The surgery and all that. Brings a human story to the whole thing.'

'I'm not sure if I'm ready to talk to a newspaper about it.' Ellie mulled the idea over for a moment: she wasn't sure if it felt comfortable. 'Can't one of you do it?'

'We can if you want.' Petra squeezed Ellie's hand. 'No pressure. I do think it would be a better story coming from you, but you shouldn't do it if it makes you uncomfortable. It is super personal.'

'It's *really* personal. I'm not sure I would have wanted to talk to a newspaper about my divorce so soon after it had happened,' Mara added. 'Just have a think about it, Ellie. I don't mind talking to them about the wild swim. They don't have to know that one of us had cancer. We're fundraising for cancer support – that's a common enough cause.'

'Okay.' Ellie took a drink of wine. 'I'll think about it.'

'And, by the way, I had a chat with Mark and he said he knows someone who would run a monthly bus for women up to the clinic in Truro, if we want to organise that. Saves us taking turns to drive,' Petra added. 'We can set aside some of the fundraising money to cover that for a year, if we do well.'

'Sounds good,' Clare added, and the rest of the group murmured their agreement.

'Coming through, coming through! Take care, it's hot.' Simona bustled her way to the table and placed a large tray down on a woven blue-and-white mat. 'Mushroom and spinach pizza and garlic bread, to soak up the wine.' She went over to a wooden dresser at the side of the room and took out a stack of plates with a pretty, old-fashioned floral pattern. 'Here we are. Help yourselves. I'm just going to get knives and forks.'

She busied herself in the kitchen and returned to the table with a bundle of napkins as well as the cutlery. 'Okay. Dig in, everyone.'

'This is so kind of you, Simona.' Ellie smiled up at her new friend.

'Yeah, thanks, Sim,' Clare added. 'You didn't need to feed us.'

'Ah, well, it's what I do best. No one goes hungry in this house,' Simona said, cutting the huge pizza with a sharp knife and laying the slices on the old farmhouse crockery. 'And, as I say, I'd have to roll you all out of here if we drank much more wine on empty stomachs.'

Ellie thought about all the family dinners that must have taken place at this table: all the good food, the conversation and the happy times. It was a world away from her childhood, where it had just been her and her mum. As she looked around the table, she felt thankful to be included in this group of women, each one with their own story. It was a nice feeling.

Her phone buzzed again. This time, it was Toni.

Sorry, just got your text. I've been in Morocco and the phone service was terrible. Good time to chat now?

'Sorry, ladies. I've just got to make a call.' Ellie stood up and picked up her phone. 'I won't be long.'

She wandered out to Simona's coat-filled hallway and sat on the bottom of the stairs, feeling pleasantly tipsy, and pressed Toni's picture on her phone.

'Hey. It's me,' she said, not knowing where or how to start.

'Hey, you! How *are* you, girl?' Toni's voice made Ellie smile. 'We've all been so worried about you.'

'I'm okay,' Ellie began. 'Toni? I wanted to ask you... Did I push you away? All you guys? I didn't mean to, if I did. I just wanted to say I'm sorry. I spoke to someone recently, and he said I could be kind of an ice queen. Do you think of me that way? An ice queen?' Ellie declined to mention that the person who had used the phrase was Rowland Hyatt. Toni would ask her a thousand questions about Rowland if she did, starting with whether they were getting back together.

'Oh my gawwwd, Ellie. Please don't apologise when you're the one who's recovering from cancer.' Toni was one of those people who found it impossible to be totally serious at any time, but Ellie thought this was as grown-up as she'd ever heard her. 'Yeah, you can be hard to read. And I'm sorry if I kind of didn't know how to talk to you about this. But I'm here for you, okay? We're all here for you.'

'Thank you.' Ellie choked back a sob.

'Totally. So, tell me: what's the man situation like in Cornwall? And what's the shopping like? Come on. The important stuff, yah.'

Ellie knew Toni was joking; it was her way. But she also knew that Toni cared about her.

'Okay.' Ellie started telling her about Magpie Cove. About Marilyn, and the beach house, and the Wild Sisterhood and all the rest of it. It felt good, and Ellie wondered how close she had come to letting her friendship with Toni and the rest of them slip altogether. Ironically, it seemed that by letting one group of people into her world and her heart, it had made it easier for her to mend the bonds she had with her other friends.

Not for the first time, Ellie thanked whatever fate it was that had brought her to Magpie Cove. And when she put the phone down, promising to call Toni later for a longer chat, she replied impulsively to Rowland's text, which read:

Dinner, drinks and dancing at one of Cornwall's finest establishments. Wednesday night. Dress code: Sexy Ice Queen.

Ellie shook her head. Rowland definitely wasn't holding back. She tapped out a reply and pressed Send before she could persuade herself not to.

Love to. Come and get me at seven. IQ xx PS... I assume that's just the dress code for me?

He replied immediately.

Good. Yes, I will be the James Bond to your Xenia Onatopp.

She chuckled to herself. It was time to live, and she should say yes to every opportunity. Even dinner and dancing with Rowland, a man with questionable taste in films.

I'm impressed you didn't say Octopussy, she replied, smiling to herself.

Believe me, I thought about it, his text came back, and Ellie laughed aloud.

TWENTY-ONE

Ellie was almost asleep when a loud noise woke her.

She sat up in bed, her heart beating.

Bang bang bang bang. It was the front door. She looked at her watch: it was just after midnight.

'What the...?' Ellie muttered to herself, grabbing her fluffy bathrobe and putting it on as she rushed out into the small hallway at the top of the stairs.

Fee came out of her room, rubbing her eyes. 'What the hell's that noise?' she muttered. 'Made me jump out of my skin.'

'It's the door.' Ellie flinched as the banging reverberated through the beach house again. They both crept downstairs.

'Get a frying pan.' Fee pointed to the kitchen, and picked up a vase from the top of the fireplace.

'Fee, if someone was going to break in, I doubt they'd knock,' Ellie whispered, but she ran to the kitchen anyway and picked up a wok.

Fee unlocked the door and swung it open, vase at the ready.

Ellie switched the downstairs light on just as Jamey rushed in.

'You've got to hide me. He's after me!' Jamey cried, standing in the middle of the beach house living room, waving her arms. 'Shut the door! Quick!'

'What's going on? Who are you?' Fee slammed the front door.

'Jamey, what's happening?' Ellie dropped the pan on the sofa and approached Jamey as if a scared animal had just burst into the house. 'Hey. Calm down. It's okay.'

'Darren. Thank God the kids are at my mum's. Banging on my front door, drunk. I went out the back, but he'd come round the side and I didn't see him. Caught me by the hair but I got away. Ran down to the beach. I think I dodged him, but I didn't know where else to go,' she panted.

Ellie made her sit down, and lifted up her blonde ponytail gently. 'Ouch. Jamey, he's pulled out quite a lot of hair.' Ellie frowned. Jamey's scalp was bleeding, and Ellie knew that she'd had a lucky escape. Goodness only knew what Darren would have done if Jamey hadn't got away.

'I'm calling the police.' Fee's tone was grim as she tapped 999 into her phone.

Jamey reached up her hand to the back of her head and looked at the blood on her hand. She started to cry.

'Oh, Jamey.' Ellie gave the girl a gentle hug, as Jamey sobbed into her shoulder. 'I'm so sorry this is happening to you.'

'He was so sweet to me,' Jamey sobbed. 'When we started goin' out. He always opened doors for me. Bought me presents. Told me I was b... b... beautiful.' She leaned heavily on Ellie's shoulder. 'I'm scared, Ellie. He won't leave me alone.'

'Fee's calling the police,' Ellie said, calmly. 'It's going to be all right.'

'On hold,' Fee muttered, walking into the kitchen. 'Must be a busy night.'

'Okay. Well, why don't we make some hot chocolate in the meantime?' Ellie maintained her calm voice. 'I think you could do with something sweet for the—' She was going to say *shock*, but there was a crash, and something came flying through the window. Glass splintered everywhere.

'What the...' Ellie cowered, instinctively covering Jamey's body with her own as the jagged rock slid to the edge of the sofa. It was from the beach outside: there were a million like it.

'Jamey!' Darren's voice screamed, outside the house. 'Come out, you stupid bitch! You're my wife! You can't hide from me!'

'Oh, my God.' Jamey cowered on the sofa. 'I thought I lost him.'

Ellie swore, and ran to the door to lock it. She had just slid the chain across and flicked the old iron bolts inside the door when she felt a thud, as Darren hit the door with his full body weight. She screamed.

'Fee, get Jamey upstairs,' she shouted. 'And stay on the line to the police!'

Fee and Jamey ran up the stairs obediently. Ellie whirled around, looking for any other easy entrances to the house. There was a wooden back door that led off the kitchen, but she knew it was locked. However, she could see that the key was in the lock, and there was a glass panel in the door that could mean someone could break the glass and reach down for the key to open it.

Ellie ran to the kitchen, made sure the door was locked and then pulled out the key. She didn't have any way of securing the glass, but she pulled the heavy pine kitchen table up to the door and wedged it against it as best she could. She couldn't do anything about the broken window either, but she hoped that Darren wasn't crazy enough to try climbing in through it, given the jagged glass that remained in the frame.

However, she wasn't ready to give him the benefit of the doubt.

As Ellie stood next to the sofa, wondering what to do and whether Fee had got through to the police yet, another rock came crashing through the beach house's other front window. Ellie ducked behind the sofa.

'Come out, bitch!' Darren slurred. *At least if he's drunk, he might pass out,* Ellie thought, aware that it was reasonably unlikely. But at this point, she'd take any unlikely circumstance that would mean Darren would stop battering the beach house, and scaring her to death.

She looked around in desperation for anything that could help her, hearing Darren muttering to himself and pacing around to the side of the house. In the kitchen she grabbed a carving knife from the rack on the counter, then ran back to the sofa with it. She hoped she didn't have to use it, but she wasn't about to face Darren empty-handed.

The back door rattled and the handle twisted. Ellie yelped and ran to the bottom of the stairs.

'Fee! Have you spoken to the police yet?' she shouted.

Jamey appeared at the top of the stairs, tear-streaked mascara running down her face.

'She's talking to them now. They're sending someone,' she hissed. 'Is he down there still?'

'Yeah.' Ellie darted a glance at the back door. 'Stay up there, okay?'

Jamey bit her lip, her arms crossed across her chest. 'Okay.'

There was a thud as Darren hurled himself at the back door, and then a noise that Ellie couldn't identify. *Thud. Crack. Crack.* She realised after a moment that he was hurling the terracotta pots filled with geraniums, roses and delphiniums onto the wooden deck of the porch.

Mara's going to be so angry when she sees what this lout's done to her house, Ellie thought. She was scared, but she was also furious that Darren had frightened her, and furious that he was ruining Mara's beautiful beach house. Ellie looked down at the carving knife in her hand and knew it wouldn't be enough to scare him off: he was drunk and violent. He'd be just as likely to run at her as run away if she waved it at him.

But she had to do something. She couldn't just listen to him destroy everything, ranting and raving around the outside of the house like a bear on a rampage.

Just for a moment, Ellie wished she had a gun. Not that anyone in England really had guns, apart from the police, or farmers sometimes had them. Criminals had them, of course. But, in that moment, she imagined going out onto the beach house porch with a rifle or a shotgun, firing a warning shot over his head and inflicting a tiny proportion of the fear that Darren was currently inflicting on her, Jamey and Fee, on him.

However, short of running upstairs and dropping an anvil that she didn't possess on Darren from one of the bedroom windows, Ellie didn't have anything that she could use to get rid of him.

It had gone quiet outside. Ellie heard a sound that might have been Darren jumping off the porch, and peered cautiously out of the window. At the end of the beach, the blue lights of the local police car lit up the cove in a spectral glow. She watched as Darren ran off, down the beach and towards the rocky headland opposite. She knew that there was nowhere to go, that way. With the tide in, as it currently was, you couldn't get anywhere other than up a sheer rock promontory that shielded a few houses on the other side. Ellie doubted that Darren, drunk, would have much chance at it in the dark, and with the rock slick with sea water.

She called Jamey and Fee down, and they watched the two police officers run after him. Yet, oddly, despite them seeming to search the beach for a long time, he seemed to have escaped their grasp.

'It's all right. He's gone.' Ellie held Jamey's hand, which was shaking.

'He's not going to leave me alone. Even with a restraining

order.' Jamey shuddered. 'I don't know what I'm gonna do. I'm so scared.'

Fee went to the cleaning cupboard and came back with a broom and swept up the glass.

'Well, we're going to need to let Mara know about the damage,' she said. 'I guess she's got insurance. Just the windows, is it?'

'I think so.' Ellie got out her phone. 'I'd better text her. I don't want to wake her up.'

'Okay. I think we need a drink in the meantime. And I don't mean hot chocolate this time.' Fee blew out her cheeks. 'That was scary.'

'I think there's some brandy in the cupboard.' Ellie pointed, walking into the kitchen. 'I'd feel happier if they'd caught him, though.'

'I'm gonna call Mark.' Jamey tapped her phone, wiping her eyes. 'Thank God the kids were at my mum's. Thank God.'

There was a knock at the door. 'Police,' said a thick Cornish accent. 'You all right in there?'

'I'll get it.' Fee handed Jamey a tumbler half-full with brandy and knocked one back herself. 'I think it's going to be a long night.'

TWENTY-TWO

Ellie didn't think that she could go back to sleep after the police had left, but she'd gone up to her room and lain down on the bed. Jamey had taken the sofa, and Fee was in her room once more. She must have more or less passed out from exhaustion – her recovery still left her easily tired – because when she woke up to the smell of smoke her clock read 4 a.m.

Ellie blinked, trying to focus in the dark room. Was she imagining the smell of smoke?

No. It was definitely there. She pushed her window open further, rubbing her eyes blearily. Maybe someone was having a bonfire on the beach. But no one was there. Yet, there was a definite burning smell.

I'm just not meant to get any sleep tonight, I guess, Ellie thought as she stumbled onto the landing and went downstairs. But as soon as she walked into the lounge, all of her sleepiness disappeared.

The beach house was on fire.

Ellie grabbed a tea towel, ran it under the tap and held it in front of her face, then went back for another one, ran to the sofa and thrust it in Jamey's face.

'Jamey. Wake up. Jamey!'

For a moment, Ellie panicked that Jamey had inhaled too much smoke, but then her eyelids fluttered open with a confused expression. She was just a deep sleeper, Ellie supposed.

'What?' Jamey muttered, and then coughed. Smoke hovered in the room like grey ribbon, and Ellie could see that it was getting thicker as the seconds passed. She ran to the front door, struggled with the security chain and the bolts that she had been so glad of just hours earlier, and finally pushed it open.

'Come on! Quickly!' Ellie rushed Jamey out onto the beach. 'Call 999!' she shouted. From outside, she could see that the fire had started at the back of the beach house and was licking up the sides of the wooden walls fast. 'I'm going back in for Fee.'

'You can't go back in!' Jamey grabbed at Ellie's flimsy cotton vest top, but she pulled free.

'Call the fire brigade. I have to,' she repeated, and ran back inside the house.

Inside, the smoke was heavier already and Ellie felt it infiltrate her lungs immediately. She held the tea towel over her face and tried to take as small breaths as possible.

She ran up the stairs and found Fee lying on the floor of the landing. The smoke was thick up here now too.

'Fee! Come on. Time to walk. Wake up!' she yelled at her friend, but Fee was only half aware of where she was. 'Okay. Okay,' she muttered under her breath, coughing.

Ellie knelt down, put her hands under Fee's arms and started to drag her towards the stairs.

There was no time to consider whether dragging someone down the stairs was a sensible idea or not. But Ellie knew she had no choice. She couldn't wait until the fire brigade got to them.

She summoned as much strength as she could and started to

manoeuvre Fee down the stairs. Ellie's arms and back screamed with pain, but she kept going. She couldn't think about her own injuries now.

Finally, she got to the bottom of the stairs, and started to drag Fee to the open door. The smoke was filling her lungs and she was feeling faint. *Just a little further*, she thought, crazily, feeling disconnected from her body. *Just a little further, and this will all be over*.

The door was so close, but it felt like miles. The distance telescoped into a long corridor in front of her eyes. *Just a little further*.

Ellie closed her eyes, tiredness overtaking her. She could hear herself coughing, but it was as if it was someone else, far away. She could feel the sea air through the front door occasionally buffeting her skin. *That's nice*, she thought, as she fell into a deep unconsciousness. *Sea air is so good for you*.

And as she floated away, Ellie remembered what it had been like in the moment before the anaesthetic kicked in, before her surgery. She remembered the doctor, before, telling her they would make her look normal again. Telling her that survival rates were good.

Survival rates.

You'll look normal again, don't worry.

You'll survive.

The phrases were like smoke in her dream, weaving in and out of each other.

Ellie floated, above the beach house, in the ocean of the sky.

TWENTY-THREE

Ellie awoke to the beeping of hospital machines for the second time in six months.

She coughed. Her throat felt like it was lined with soot.

Weakly, her eyes fluttered open.

A nurse looked over from the other side of a sunny room, painted yellow. 'Oh, hello! You're awake,' she said, coming over to Ellie's bed.

'What happened?' Ellie whispered. She tried to clear her throat, but it wouldn't clear.

'Careful. You need to keep the oxygen mask on for now.' The nurse adjusted the straps holding the mask to Ellie's face. 'Do you remember? You were in a fire. You saved your friend who was there too.' She indicated the bed next to Ellie, where Fee lay with her eyes closed and an oxygen mask on her face.

'Oh, no. Fee!' Ellie tried to get up, but fell back on her pillows. 'Is she... will she be all right?'

'You both inhaled smoke, but the fire brigade got to you pretty quickly. The other girl that was there with you, they said she tried to go back in for you, but she couldn't stand the smoke. Fortunately for you, you'd dragged Fiona near to the open door so you had that air coming in. That's probably what saved you.' The nurse patted her hand. 'They're going to keep you in for a bit, monitor you. We have to keep an eye on your heart, and make sure you don't get any infections. Especially you, as you've had surgery recently.'

'I feel like death warmed up,' Ellie whispered.

'I know. Rest, fluids, and we'll make sure you're okay. If you give us the details of whoever did your mastectomy, we'll get in touch with them as well.'

'Okay.' Ellie felt exhausted just from that brief interaction. She turned her head carefully to look at Fee in the next bed.

'She hasn't woken up yet?' she whispered, hoarsely.

'No. But I expect she will soon. I think she inhaled more smoke than you did, from what the other girl at the scene told the fire brigade.' The nurse put her hand on Ellie's forehead; it was a reassuring gesture. 'Don't worry. Try not to, anyway.'

Ellie closed her eyes. It was impossible not to worry. What if Fee didn't recover? What if her efforts in pulling her best friend from a burning building were all for nothing? She felt useless, hopeless. Tears welled in her eyes.

'Oh, darling. It's going to be okay.' The nurse handed Ellie a tissue. 'You just woke up in hospital. You're going to feel low and crappy right now. Okay? But in a few days you'll feel a lot better, I promise. Try to rest. Here – drink some water.' She handed Ellie a plastic beaker half full with water. 'We've got you an IV for now, too. It's all being taken care of.'

Ellie sipped the water; her mouth tasted like charcoal. She felt fatigue overcome her again, and her eyes began to close.

Behind her eyelids, the starry night sky of Magpie Cove beckoned her: slipping into a fractured dream, she found herself flying over the rooftops of the village again. But, this time, the beach house was burning, and there was nothing she could do to stop it.

TWENTY-FOUR

When Ellie woke again, Fee was sitting up in bed next to her, eating a yoghurt and watching TV.

'Oh, thank goodness. You're alive,' Ellie whispered in her hoarse voice.

'Morning, sleepy.' Fee turned to her and reached her arm out of bed towards Ellie's bed. Ellie carefully reached her own arm out to meet Fee's hand, brushing her fingers lightly. ''Course I'm alive. Thanks to you.' She finished the yoghurt and replaced the oxygen mask over her face. 'Throat feels like I've been on fifty a day, though.' She coughed, scowling at the sensation.

'Same here.' Ellie blinked, focusing on her surroundings again. 'How long was I out?'

'Dunno. I woke up in the night and you were out cold until now.' Fee's voice was as scratchy as Ellie's. 'Nurse says it's going to be a few days until we can go, all being well.'

'I woke up and you were unconscious. I must have passed out again.' Ellie tried to sit up, but a jolt of pain sliced through her skull. 'Oh, my head.' She pressed her hands to her forehead.

'Headache is normal, apparently,' Fee said, huskily. 'Mine's passing a bit now.'

'What the hell happened? I mean, the fire?' Ellie found a remote control attached to the bed and set the back of her bed more upright. 'It didn't start inside the house. I'm sure of that.'

'No. It was from the outside.' Fee closed her eyes and lay back on her pillow. 'The nurse told me. I reckon it was Darren. Coming back to have another go.'

'Darren? But why would he do that?' Ellie coughed.

'Why wouldn't he? He'd already hammered the doors and broken the windows.'

'God. Maybe. Is Jamey okay?'

'Yeah. You got her out pretty quickly, I think. I don't think she's here, anyway.' Fee took a sip of water from her plastic beaker.

'The nurse told me she tried to help us but the smoke was too much,' Ellie added.

'Fair enough. You pulled her out, she was right to stay out.'

'Hello, hello... ready for visitors?' Mara opened the door to Fee and Ellie's room, holding a huge bunch of flowers and a carrier bag.

'Hi, Mara.' Ellie coughed. 'Come in.'

'You poor sausages.' Mara set the bunch of flowers down on a table in the corner and stood between the beds. 'I can't believe what happened. Are you okay? I mean, obviously you're not okay, but you know what I mean. I brought your phones, by the way. I found them in the house and thought you'd want them. They seem all right, not that I've been nosy or anything.' She handed both of them a phone, and pulled a charger out of her bag. 'Thought you might need to charge them too.'

'Oh, you're amazing. Thank you. We're okay. I think.' Fee coughed again. 'Excuse the coughing. We've got sooty lungs at the moment.'

'Oh, it's just terrible.' Mara sat down on the edge of Fee's bed, facing Ellie. 'I'm so sorry. I feel somehow responsible.'

'How are you responsible? It's your house that was on fire. How damaged is it – if you don't mind me asking?' Ellie rasped.

'It could be worse. The back of the house is brick up to a certain point, as you know, and then wood. Seems whoever set light to it – and the fire brigade definitely think it was arson – set a fire onto the wood.' She shook her head, blinking.

Ellie could see that Mara was trying to hold back her feelings, but she was clearly upset. Of course she was upset. It was hardly surprising.

'Ah, look at me, coming to see you both in hospital and going on about the house. I brought you some snacks and drinks too.' Mara took out some chocolates, cans of fizzy drinks and a large paper bag with 'Maude's Fine Buns' printed on the side.

'So... how much damage is there?' Fee prompted, gently.

'It's mostly the kitchen. We'll need to put a whole new one in, again. It just seems like five minutes ago we restored it in the first place.' Mara sighed. 'Other than that, it's mostly smoke damage. Most of the furniture will have to be replaced. I mean, we're insured, so it'll be fine. But it's more the sentimental value of some of those things.' She sighed again. 'The thing is, I love that house. But in some ways, it's kind of cursed. I mean, not literally. But bad things happened to my mum there. Not specifically in the house, but nearby, I think. And she was unhappy there, afterwards.'

'I'm sorry,' Ellie squeaked. She took a drink of water.

'Yeah. Magpie Cove's a funny place. On one hand, loads of brilliant things happen here. People come here and change their lives completely. But...'

'But what?'

'Hmm. It's hard to describe. I guess what I mean is that there are shadows here too. Take my mum. You know you found that box at the beach house, with the letters inside?'

'Oh, yeah!' Fee picked up the paper bag from Maude's bakery and looked inside. She took out an iced doughnut and started to eat it ravenously. 'What was that all about?'

'Well, as I think I explained, Mum had me when she was a teenager. She didn't want to get pregnant, let's just say. She was attacked.' Mara raised an eyebrow.

'You mean...?' Ellie was horrified.

'Yeah. Anyway, I never knew, and I still don't know the details other than what she wrote in a diary at the time. I found that in the beach house when she died and left it to me. I didn't know who did it. Who my biological father was. Or is.'

'And those letters have that information?' Ellie probed.

'They do.'

'Oh, my goodness. Who was it, then?'

'It was a friend of the family. His name was Alton Robb.'

'Do you know him? Does he still live here?' Fee gasped.

'I don't know him, no. But there is a Robb family in the village. They're one of the ones that go back generations. I've done some subtle asking around, and Alton Robb passed away a year ago. He wasn't that old, but he had early onset dementia, apparently.' Mara exhaled a long breath.

'That was your father,' Ellie wheezed, then coughed. 'Sorry.'

'Technically, yes. He was my biological father. And a rapist,' Mara snapped.

'Wow. That's... difficult,' Fee said, quietly. 'I'm so sorry, Mara.'

'I didn't mean to sound angry with you. I mean, I am angry. But with him. With them.'

'Oh, no.' Ellie breathed. 'He was here the whole time.'

'He was.' Mara stared at the TV for a moment, which Fee had muted. On the screen, an advert showed a man ecstatically mopping a kitchen floor. 'It's messed up. And, in a weird way, it feels like the beach house catching fire and me finding that out are somehow connected. Like, do I want to continue to live in a village where I know Alton's family still lives? Did they know what he did? I don't know.'

'Yes, I can see why you'd wonder about that. And it must feel weird.' Fee shivered.

'Yeah. I don't know what to do about the beach house. We'll restore it, but then I might finally sell it. I was going to originally, and then Brian and I fell in love and we decided to keep it. A lot of that was for sentimental reasons; about the time we spent there together when we first met. But now... we might move out of the village. Sell up, make a new start somewhere else. St Ives, maybe.'

'I'm so sorry, Mara.' Ellie reached for her hand. 'I just feel like we could have done something. But I don't know what.'

'You couldn't have done anything!' Mara patted her hand. 'Really and truly. I'm just so relieved everyone is still alive. It looks bad for Darren Chivers, though, let me tell you. That low-life scum.' Mara's eyes narrowed. 'I hope they throw away the key. It's bad enough what he did to my house, but Mark told me all about what he's done to poor Jamey and the kids. Men like that don't deserve mercy.'

'Is Jamey okay?' Fee asked.

'She's okay physically, Mark says. Bit of a mess otherwise, as you can imagine, but he's looking after her and the kids. He asked after you.' Mara tapped Ellie on the knee. 'I told him to come and see you, but he was being shy about it. He said he thought you had enough to deal with. I told him to get over himself.'

'Oh.' Ellie wheezed under her oxygen mask. 'Please tell me he's not coming. I look like crap.'

'You are so vain.' Fee tried to laugh, but it came out as a choked noise.

'I'm serious. I feel and look like hell. I do not want

gentlemen visitors.' Ellie accepted a can of fizzy fruit juice from Mara.

'Fair enough. But you should text him, in that case. He's worried about you,' Mara chided. 'We all are.'

'I was supposed to go out with Rowland.' Ellie drank from her can carefully. The bubbles made her cough, so she put it down. 'Has he been in? While I was asleep?'

'No, but I don't think many people have yet. The nurse said people have left loads of messages and phoned to check up on us. Probably want to leave us in peace a bit.' Fee took a sip of water and groaned. 'Agh. My chest is so sore,'

'I should text him.' Ellie picked up her phone and pressed the button: thankfully, the screen lit up. It still had some charge, and she could see lots of texts and message notifications. Two texts were from Rowland, all in capitals:

OH MY GOD I JUST HEARD, ARE YOU OKAY?

I'M COMING TO THE HOSPITAL

There were messages from the Wild Sisterhood, which she read aloud to Fee. And there were a couple of messages from Mark, hoping she felt okay and sending his love.

Ellie's heart flipped a little as she read that one. She replied:

Okay, thanks. Feel pretty yuck but they think we'll be okay. Send baked goods.

She watched the screen in hope for a few moments, but Mark wasn't a fast replier. He was usually working, and probably had his head in an engine with his phone in another room.

Instead, she replied to Rowland, who replied immediately with a shower of emojis.

Words would have been nice, she thought, seeing as she'd

been in a life-threatening incident, but maybe Rowland was busy, and it was nice of him to reply at all.

She closed her eyes, feeling a wave of fatigue engulf her. She dropped the phone onto her covers. *I'll get it later*, she thought, woozily, drifting off. It was too much to focus on anything for too long right now.

But when she dreamed, it was Mark she saw, not Rowland. In her sleep, she smiled.

TWENTY-FIVE

'Well, here she is. All done, finally.' Mark rubbed a spot of something only he could see from Marilyn's shining silver façade.

'It's all fixed, then? We can drive her again?' Ellie opened Marilyn's driver's side door and peered inside. She and Fee were more or less back to normal now, but she still felt a little weak. The doctors had let them leave hospital, and they had to go back to London.

'Yup. Valeted her inside as well. You all right?' He looked concerned as Ellie coughed. 'I came to see you at the hospital. But you were asleep.'

'Yeah, I'm okay. Thank you,' she said, feeling awkward in his presence. If he was Rowland, he'd be halfway through some long anecdote about Marilyn Monroe by now. Ellie thought back to what Esther had said at their dinner at Simona's house: *If he's a man of few words, the ones he does say are all the more important.* 'Thanks for visiting. Sorry I wasn't awake.'

'That's okay. I left you some bread I made.' He gave her a brief smile. 'Seein' as you like it so much.'

'Oh, right. Yeah, that was amazing,' Ellie chuckled. 'We

shared it with the nurses. We had it with soup.' The bread had been a soft white bloomer, a thoughtful touch, since Ellie's and Fee's throats were raw. Anything tough like a crusty sourdough would have been impossible to eat.

'You're welcome.' He looked away shyly.

'So, Marilyn looks beautiful,' Ellie changed the subject.

'That carpet hadn't seen a deep clean since the 80s, I reckon,' he added, quietly.

Ellie caught his eye; she thought she detected a sparkle in his voice, but he was poker-faced.

'Mark, thank you *so, so much,'* Fee told him enthusiastically. 'You're our knight in shining armour. Or our knight in shining motorhome, anyway. Marilyn looks so good! Have you cleaned her on the outside too?' Fee walked along Marilyn's length, making appreciative noises. 'Look, Ellie! There used to be a dent here. It's gone!'

'She's a piece of vintage. Got to look after her.' Mark shrugged bashfully. 'Too many old things getting ruined. Makes you want to look after what you can.'

The fire at the beach house had affected everyone, it seemed. The community was in shock. Mara had said that she thought there was a shadowy side to Magpie Cove, and that was obviously true, given what Darren had done.

The police had arrested him while Ellie and Fee were in hospital. They'd come in to take their statements, and the detective had cagily suggested that they had 'identified the perpetrator using DNA evidence'. Mark had supplied the rest of the information when Ellie texted him.

It turned out that Darren, drunk, had come looking for Jamey that night despite the terms of the temporary restraining order, and had somehow managed to get some of his blood on the glass from the windows he'd broken. The fact that Ellie and Fee could identify him as being at the house and threatening them was apparently enough for the police to deduce that he had also started the fire. Plus, Darren had been found by the police later that night, still drunk, on the high street. His clothes had been stained with petrol.

'Make sure you bill me for all the work you've done, Mark. I wouldn't want to think I'd taken advantage of you just because you enjoy your work.' Ellie realised she sounded brusque, but she'd only meant it in a good way. She could imagine that Mark probably had done a lot of extra little jobs – she certainly hadn't asked him to valet the interior or bang out any dents, and she didn't like the thought of not paying him for his work.

''Twas a pleasure, Ellie,' Mark replied, softly. 'I didn't do nothing I didn't want to. I've billed you what I think's fair, in the circumstances.' He handed her a final invoice, folded in half. 'Look at it later. No rush.'

Then there were the shocking family secrets that Mara had uncovered about her origins. But there was also a wonderful side to the village: it was full of good people. Lila and Nathan, her partner, had insisted that Ellie and Fee stay at their flat in the village until they were well enough to go home. And the village was rallying round Mara and Brian, helping them repair the beach house.

Ellie opened the piece of paper. In the *Payable* box, Mark had written ZERO.

She looked up at him. 'What's this? I thought there was still a balance to pay for the final repairs. It was around two thousand.' She frowned at him.

'Nope. All paid.' Mark gave her a long stare, smiling.

'Mark, I owe you money. I know I do. We agreed it last time. I've got the last invoice here somewhere.' Ellie opened her handbag and started rifling through it.

'You don't owe me anythin'. You saved my sister's life.' Mark crossed his arms across his chest. 'End of.'

'Mark, anyone would have done the same,' Ellie protested.

'It doesn't change the fact that you've done all this work on Marilyn. I wouldn't dream of not paying you for your time.'

'You've paid me most of it.' He shrugged. 'And the rest, I'm happy to write off. Really. I mean it.' He looked uncomfortable, like he wanted to hug Ellie, but wasn't sure how to make it happen in the moment. 'Jamey's my sister. It could've gone very wrong that night. Thanks to you, it didn't,' he added.

'I... I don't know what to say.' Ellie was at a loss.

'I think what Ellie means is, that's incredibly kind, Mark,' Fee said, softly. 'Thank you.'

'You're welcome,' he replied, equally softly, never taking his eyes from Ellie's face.

'You know, I've really got used to Magpie Cove. Even after the fire. It just feels like we've been here forever,' Fee said, sadly.

'You're off, then?' Mark put his hands in his pockets.

'Tomorrow, or the day after. We're coming back for the sponsored swim, though,' Fee added.

'Oh, right. I saw the posters in the village.'

'It's going to be great! You should come.' Fee smiled. 'I bet all the girls in Magpie Cove would pay to see Mark Gardner with his top off.' She gave Mark a playful tap on the arm.

He blushed, and looked away. 'Dunno about that,' he muttered.

Fee's phone rang, and she fished it out of her pocket. 'Sorry. I've got to take this.' She gave them both a little wave. 'Talk among yourselves.'

'You sure you're okay?' Mark had a pen in his top pocket, and he took it out and turned it over in his hands. 'You sound a bit hoarse.'

'I'm okay. I have to check in with the doctor when I get back to London. They have to keep an eye on us for a bit in case we have heart problems. They don't think we will, but it can happen. Are the kids okay?'

'They'll be all right. Kids are resilient.'

'Yes, they are,' Ellie replied. There was a silence.

'You won't be here for the hearing, then. Jamey goes to court next week,' Mark added.

'No. I've got to go back to work. But I'll stay in touch with Jamey, and with Clare and Rowland. They'll let me know what's happening. Honestly, after what Darren did last week, I don't think Jamey has to worry that they won't make the restraining order permanent. He might get a custodial sentence. He should, at any rate.'

'Yeah. I hope he doesn't get to see the kids ever again. Anyway. Thank you. Again. For everything.'

'You're welcome.' Ellie gazed up into Mark's deep blue eyes. He gazed back at her with an unreadable expression on his face. For a moment, Ellie thought he was going to say something, but he cleared his throat and looked away.

'Oh my bleddy *Nora*!' Fee screamed, followed by an intense coughing fit. She'd wandered to the edge of the garage courtyard and had been talking animatedly on the phone. 'You'll never guess. I only went and got that lecturing job at Exeter University! I forgot all about it, what with all the drama.'

'What? Oh my goodness, Fee! That's amazing!' Ellie hugged her friend, who was jumping up and down with excitement. 'Hey. Mind my toes.'

Fee hugged Mark too, who looked taken aback but pleased.

'Gracious. Pure steel under baby soft skin,' she exclaimed as she stepped back. 'Almost enough to turn a girl. Ellie! What do you think?'

'I think it's a big change, but you should go with your heart,' Ellie said. 'What's your instinct about it?'

'Oh, gawd. I think I want it.' Fee made a face. 'Do you hate me?'

'I could never hate you!' Ellie laughed.

'Congratulations!' Mark grinned. 'You not going back with Ellie, then?'

'Oh, I'll go back. The job doesn't start until September, and I have to respond formally with a yes or no. I said I'd let them know within a week.' Fee twirled around. 'Argh! Exciting! I'd have to pack up my flat in London. Or let it out, I don't know. There's so much to think about!'

'I didn't know you were so excited about it.' Ellie was happy for Fee, but the thought of not having her in London made her sad. She'd hardly see Fee if she was in Exeter.

'I didn't think I had much of a chance, not having any university experience.' Fee danced on the spot. 'And we just really ended up having a chat when I went in. I didn't think much more of it. But, yeah. I really liked the idea of it all along.'

'Well. On that bombshell, I guess we should be going.' Ellie looked around at the garage. 'We can talk about it on the way home. Look at you. You're as giddy as a goat.'

'That is such a Cornish phrase. You've been here too long.' Fee planted a kiss on Mark's cheek. 'Mark Gardner, take care of yourself and your family. Don't be a stranger. Come and see us in London or something.'

'Right you are.' He handed Ellie Marilyn's keys. 'That's that, then,' he muttered. 'Pleasure knowing you, Ellie,' he added, in a husky voice, and turned away.

Ellie felt an unexpected pull of regret in her chest, like she was losing something she had never quite had – something special, that was meant for her. But Mark Gardner had just been a passing acquaintance in this unexpected episode of her life: life was about to go back to normal, and soon, Magpie Cove would just be a memory.

That was all it was.

'And you,' she said, quietly.

TWENTY-SIX

Ellie was in her bedroom on board Marilyn, folding the clothes she'd just picked up from a local launderette. Most of her clothes had just needed a good wash to get the smoke out, since the fire itself hadn't got to the bedrooms of the beach house. She'd had to buy some new shoes in the village, though.

There was a knock on the door.

'Just a minute!' she yelled, looking around for some jeans; she was currently in her knickers and a vest top with her hair pulled into a messy bun.

Fee had gone over to St Ives in a taxi to take a portfolio of work over to a client – fortunately, her laptop and the printer hadn't been affected by the smoke. They had driven Marilyn out of Mark's garage and onto the small stretch of road that overlooked the cove, just for the night. They'd be off in the morning, but Mark needed the space for another repair he had coming in. It was fair enough, Fee pointed out: Marilyn had dominated his garage for weeks.

Since it was such a hot night, and since she was so close by, Ellie had been considering going for one final dip in the sea when she'd finished sorting out all her stuff – once it got darker and there was no one around at the beach.

Despite everything that had happened, she was definitely going to miss waking up to the soft sound of the waves crashing in the cove, and the bright sunlight that glowed through her curtains every morning. It was sad to see the beach house in such a bad way. Everything stank, and the once-bright white curtains and bed linen in Ellie's room had been stripped away and replaced. There was no saving any soft furnishings after a fire, it seemed. Ellie wished that her last memories of the beach house could be as it used to be: cosy and stylish. Now, she would forever think of it as damaged.

She pulled on some loose shorts and a short-sleeved summer hoodie, and answered the door.

Mark Gardner stood outside the motorhome, his hands in his pockets. The sun was setting over the beach, cerise evening light reflected in the water, merging air and ocean together in a fiery marriage.

'Oh. Hi,' Ellie breathed. Whoever she'd been expecting, it wasn't Mark.

'Ellie. I...' He trailed off. 'I had to... I couldn't just let you leave without...'

'Without what?' she said, softly, into the silence that followed. She could see he was fighting with himself; trying to find the right thing to say.

Her eyes travelled over his strong chin, his soft eyes. Ellie remembered the electricity of Mark's gaze that day at the beach, when he had looked back at her across the sand, seeming to hear her desire for him. Despite the distance, in that moment she had felt that look in every secret part of her body.

He was looking at her again in just the same way. And it made her feel exactly the same as before: as if she was melting.

Without answering, Mark stepped forward and kissed her.

This time, Ellie didn't push him away. Instead, she wrapped her arms around his neck and surrendered to his lips on hers.

So this is what people mean when they talk about having chemistry, she thought, briefly, before she was consumed by the moment.

Ellie had kissed her share of men, and it was nice. Exciting, often. But kissing Mark was something else entirely. It was as though there was something in their physical connection that was every single cliché in all the romantic songs she'd heard. There was a sense of fitting together perfectly, of a deep desire, an energy between them that felt both right and comfortable.

When she and Mark had gone out, she'd pushed him away out of fear. And, because of fear, she had missed out on this.

Kissing Mark Gardner made Ellie feel alive. But it was more than that: kissing Mark made Ellie feel right in her skin again. It was a feeling she hadn't had for a long time.

Suddenly, the balance of their relationship shifted from an unacknowledged attraction and all their jokey conversations to some other plane, where their bodies and souls connected effortlessly.

Breaking the kiss for a moment, Ellie took Mark's hand. She led him into the motorhome, letting her instinct finally break free and take over.

'Are you sure you want to do this?' Mark murmured. 'I didn't expect... I mean, I just wanted to see you before you go.'

'I want this. Do you?' Ellie met his hungry gaze.

'Yes,' he answered simply, kissing her again.

'Come on, then.' Ellie led Mark to her bedroom, feeling like a teenager. Sometimes, these moments came – though they had been few and far between in Ellie's life so far – where fate seemed to take over. She could feel that energy between her and Mark now: a magical, perfect time where life seemed to be saying, *Take this precious time together now. This is your moment.*

'I was scared I'd lost you. In the fire,' he murmured as he held her close. 'I should have been there, and I wasn't.'

'You couldn't have known.' Ellie traced the line of his chin with her fingertip. 'It was an accident. Out of the blue.'

'I should have been there,' he repeated, stubbornly.

'You're here now,' she breathed, and he smiled as he kissed her again.

Outside her window, the sun was setting quickly, and the light was fading. In her room, Ellie pulled Mark to the bed. Warm light made a protective glow around them as, slowly, Mark unzipped Ellie's hoodie, pushed her vest top down and gently kissed the scar that had brought her to Magpie Cove.

'Let's make the most of it, then,' he replied.

TWENTY-SEVEN

SIX WEEKS LATER

Ellie awoke to the sound of seagulls, and opened her eyes groggily against a shaft of light. She sat up in bed and pushed the curtain aside.

The sun was rising over the sea in Magpie Cove, and Ellie wondered if she had ever seen a sunrise as magnificent. It was as if a cup of molten, jewelled amber was being poured on the sky, with broad sweeps of orange at the horizon. Ellie took in a deep breath.

It was good to be back.

Ellie had spent almost six weeks back at work, and she couldn't say that she had enjoyed being back in London much at all. She still liked her job, but there was no way that she could keep up with her previous crazy schedule of dawn runs along the Thames, or being in the gym by six thirty in the morning, and at her desk by seven forty-five.

If I'm going to be awake at six thirty, she thought to herself as she snuggled in the warm duvet she had added to Marilyn's main bedroom, *then I'd much rather be watching the sunrise at Magpie Cove from a vintage motorhome, any day of the week.*

Ellie also had to admit that, though she would always love

working in the legal profession, she had realised since she'd been back that corporate law was no longer for her. She just didn't care about it as much as she once had. It all seemed rather pointless and impersonal.

Wrapping a fluffy robe around her, she tiptoed along Marilyn's hallway and opened the side door of the motorhome, stepping down carefully onto the tarmac of the small road at the edge of the beach where they had parked up the night before.

The cove was completely deserted, although Ellie could see that the girls had been busy getting it ready for the sponsored wild swim: bunting hung from what seemed like every available nook and cranny; there was a Portakabin at the edge of the beach with a sign outside it where people could come and pay to take part; and there were already some food trucks lined up along the road from Marilyn, ready to fill up hungry post-swim stomachs with Cornish pasties, cakes, vegan wraps and ice creams.

It was as though Magpie Cove had been waiting for her while she was away.

Ellie took in a deep breath of the sea air, grateful for the way it made her feel calm and centred. Her cough had almost entirely gone now: occasionally, she felt a rasp in her lungs, but it was minimal. Her doctor in London had insisted that she went in for weekly check-ups, and had told her very specifically that she had to avoid doing crazy long hours in the office.

She wondered how the repairs on the beach house were getting on: it certainly looked back to normal from the outside, but from where she was she could only see the front. It felt strange that, for a while, it had seemed like home; she could almost see the ghost of herself sitting on the rocking chair on the porch.

And, of course, she could hardly forget that last night in Magpie Cove. Her heart beat faster as she thought of how Mark had made her feel: how he had looked at her as she lay naked next to him. How he had touched her with a gentleness that she didn't think she had ever experienced before – and the fiery hot desire that had engulfed her in pleasure.

He had told her that he didn't care about her mastectomy. That she was beautiful exactly as she was; the most beautiful woman he'd ever known. If he hadn't known it before the fire, he said, then how he'd felt when he thought he might have lost her was more than clear.

At the time, she'd said, *You don't have to say that.* But he held her in his strong arms and looked deep in her eyes and said, *What do I have to do to convince you? I mean, I would have thought that all this would be obvious enough.*

It is, it is. I'm sorry. She had kissed him then, still not quite believing what had happened.

Ellie had been thinking about Magpie Cove a lot whilst she was back in London, replaying that night with Mark over and over in her mind.

She'd fallen asleep in his arms, afterwards, but when she'd woken up as the sun streamed in the window the next morning, he was gone. He had left her a note:

I wish we had more time. I'll miss you.

But that was all.

She'd run to the garage the next morning to say goodbye, but he wasn't there. One of his assistants had mumbled something about Mark having to take the rescue truck down the coast to pick someone up who had broken down. Ellie hadn't known whether that was true, or whether he was avoiding her after the night before. Perhaps he felt awkward. Perhaps he thought it had been a mistake.

Ellie had texted him as Fee drove Marilyn's gleaming silver caboose carefully out of the village, but there had been no reply until the next day. His reply had been brief, and though she had stayed in touch, it was only because she had persistently texted him, and not vice versa.

Mark replied to whatever she sent – a few friendly GIFs, texts asking him how he was – but he never asked her anything or seemed to want to flirt at all. In the past couple of weeks she'd stopped getting in touch, disillusioned with feeling like she was the one doing all the work. However, she had made a point of asking him about Jamey's court case, although he had been frustratingly brief with his replies. Ellie knew that it had gone well, but not the details. Also, she was busy, and it was hard keeping up – had she really done this job every day for years?

Fee had decided to take the job in Exeter and had been busy packing up her flat. Ellie wanted to support Fee's decision, so she had worked hard at not showing her disappointment at losing her friend, but it was difficult. Fee said, after the fire, it seemed even more important to do something that made her feel alive. Ellie couldn't disagree – she understood that better than anyone.

One thing that had got her through those difficult first weeks back was a WhatsApp group that Petra had set up for everyone in the Wild Sisterhood. They'd been messaging more or less nonstop for weeks. Ellie suspected that the group were keeping tabs on her and Fee, which she appreciated, but it was also a welcome distraction from work. On one memorable occasion, Esther had messaged everyone *Oh hi my foot* which had puzzled everyone until Petra had suggested that she turn off predictive text and write it again.

When she'd read it, Ellie had to hide her grin behind her hands in an important meeting, but she was touched that Esther was getting to grips with owning her first mobile phone just so that she could be part of the group online.

Back in London, Ellie had intended to put Marilyn up for sale, but she hadn't quite managed to have the heart to do it. She'd got very attached to the huge motorhome, and, rather than sell her on, Ellie had found a large private garage not too far away where she could keep Marilyn safe and dry.

In fact, despite the owner of that garage offering her a large sum of money to buy Marilyn himself, Ellie had been spending her evenings and weekends sourcing new interior flourishes for the motorhome rather than going out for drinks. She hadn't seen her old crowd at all, apart from those she worked with; she was too tired, for one thing, and it was much nicer to spend an evening in her flat, looking up authentic 80s-style haberdashery with a glass of wine, sharing pictures of what she found with Fee and the girls.

The doctor had given her some brochures about breast reconstruction surgery on her last visit. Ellie had flicked through them, and the results did seem very good. But was she ready for more surgery? She didn't know.

Ellie had assigned that decision to herself for a couple of weeks in the future: for now, she was really looking forward to seeing the Wild Sisterhood today, and she was excited to get back in the sea again. Perhaps more than anything, Ellie had missed that regular time in the water, where she could be by herself and head off towards the horizon with just the sound of seagulls to keep her company. Had Magpie Cove healed her? She didn't know. As well as help her heal, it had hurt her too. But she was still glad that Marilyn had broken down where she had, all those weeks ago. It felt like fate.

TWENTY-EIGHT

'Beautiful day.' Rowland smiled at Ellie as she looked up from her receipt book. 'You allowed out of there for a break? You look a bit warm.'

'Rowland! Hi.' Ellie was two hours into her shift in the ticket Portakabin. It was indeed 'warm', if 'warm' was a typically Cornish understatement for 'unbearably boiling'. 'How are you?'

She'd been messaging Rowland too, on and off, since she'd been away. Rowland, in stark comparison to Mark, was a frequent and prolific correspondent, sending voice files and video as well as GIFs and emails. He made her laugh, and was always asking when she'd be back.

'All the better for seeing you, milady.' Rowland bowed theatrically. 'It's been so long. I've missed you! How is everything? Your lungs?' he enquired. 'I hope you've been resting.'

'I'm fine, thanks.' Ellie fanned herself with a nearby stack of flyers: she did feel fine, overall, but she still had weak lungs, and dreamed about the fire a lot. She hadn't mentioned it in her conversations with Rowland, because Rowland, like so many people, seemed very invested in her being well and happy –

none of which was a bad thing, of course. However, whenever she'd mentioned her dark days, Rowland hadn't responded.

'Such a shame we never got to go dancing. But I've got some plans for you, now you're back.' He gave her a confident wink.

'Oh. Well, I'm just here for the long weekend,' she demurred.

'I'm sure I can persuade you to spend some time with me,' he replied, as if it was decided.

'I expect so. Let's see,' she said, non-committally.

Ellie had got the impression that Rowland wasn't really up for listening to her talk about how traumatic the fire had been, especially after having had a mastectomy. That was Rowland: Ellie didn't think he was a bad man, just perhaps a little insensitive at times. But his heart was in the right place, and she shouldn't forget that.

'Can you get away, then?' he asked again. 'I want to give you a hug, at least!'

'Definitely. I'm waiting for Petra to take over, so when she does, I'm all yours. Are you swimming? It's £20, but that includes a T-shirt and a drink of your choice.' She held up one of the 'I CONQUERED THE COVE: MAGPIE COVE WILD SWIM 2022' T-shirts Mara had had made for participants.

Rowland handed her a £50 note. 'That's okay. I can swim here anytime, but I'm happy to contribute to a good cause.'

'Oh. Thanks! D'you want a T-shirt?' Ellie rummaged in the pile. 'We're a bit low on medium ones but I think I still have one or two.'

'What're you saying? I might be more of a large,' Rowland replied, pretending to be offended.

'Oh! Ha ha. You can have a large, if you like.' She grinned. Rowland was looking good. She knew he worked out, because he told her in gleeful detail every week how much he could bench press. And he'd clearly been at the beach a lot, because he was looking tanned. 'I just meant, because of your...' She was going to say something about him keeping so trim, but trailed off.

'Because of my what?' Rowland followed her gaze.

Behind the queue for tickets, Mark Gardner was talking to a pretty redhead with tattoos in a vest and shorts, standing by the ice-cream stall. Ellie swallowed, her tummy tensing. A vivid memory of Mark, naked, in bed with her, jumped into her mind. She wanted him to turn around and see her, but then she remembered that she had sweat running down her back, and her mascara was probably smudged all over her face. What would she say to him? What would he say to her now, after virtually ignoring her texts for the past six weeks?

'Earth to Ellie. Hey!' Rowland waved his hand in front of her face. 'If it's that much of a problem, I'll catch up with you later.' He sounded suddenly aggrieved, and his jolly tone had lost some of its sparkle. 'You've probably got a lot of people to catch up with.'

'Ummm. Yeah. I'll come and find you when I get out of here, okay?' Ellie gave Rowland the T-shirt. Seeing Mark had thrown her for a loop, and, she realised, she was also wildly jealous about the girl he was talking to. She had never been jealous, so she was slow to recognise the emotion. *He is allowed to talk to other women*, she thought. *He might be seeing someone by now. Hell, he might be married for all you know.* It would certainly explain the less-than-enthusiastic texting. But there was something primal in her that wanted to go and push the girl with the tattoos into the side of the tent.

'See you, then.' Rowland headed off, looking put out. Ellie could tell that she'd have to make it up to him and be her best and cheeriest self later – Rowland wanted to go out with her, and he'd been nothing but attentive since they'd reconnected. But all she could think about was Mark. Did she want to go out with Rowland? It was nice to have his attention, but she didn't feel as though they really connected at a deeper level.

Half an hour later, Petra arrived to take over at the Portakabin, and Ellie walked out gratefully into the sea air. It was still hot on the beach, but at least now she wasn't trapped in a metal box. Holding her Magpie Cove Wild Swim T-shirt away from her body, she flapped it in the air to dry it off as best she could.

'Hi.' Mark tapped her on the shoulder. She jumped, not having seen him come up behind her.

'Oh, gosh. Hi. Sorry. I was just...' She trailed off. 'Hot,' she finished, lamely.

'Warm day,' he agreed, lifting a baseball cap off his head and mussing his hair underneath.

'Certainly is...' she replied, feeling like a teenager. *Come on, woman*, she thought. *You're a corporate lawyer, for God's sake. Say something.*

'Friend of yours?' She looked at the girl in the ice-cream stall. Mark frowned, looking confused.

'Who?'

'That girl with the tattoos. Pretty. Red hair. Ice cream.' Ellie knew how she sounded, but it was as if an alien had temporarily taken over her brain. What was wrong with simple pleasantries? *How are you? You look well? Why didn't you ever tell me you missed me when we texted? Do you think about that night we had together – because I do?*

I think about it every night, in fact.

'No, just some girl,' he replied. Ellie raised her eyebrow and gave him a tight smile. *This has not begun well*, she thought.

'I thought you might have a new girlfriend.' The words were out before she could stop them. *This is no way to play it cool*, she rebuked herself sternly.

'I don't.' Mark frowned. There was another silence. 'I see

you brought Marilyn down.' Mark pointed at the motorhome at the end of the beach. 'She runnin' okay? Thought you were going to sell her.'

'She's perfect,' Ellie replied. 'I decided to keep her. I've been doing her up inside, in fact. You'll have to come and see.'

'I'd like that,' he replied, giving her an intense look. 'Been hopin' you'd come back,' he added.

'You knew I was coming this weekend.'

'Yeah. But still...' He met her eyes and then looked away at the swimmers. 'I... um. I think about you a lot. About that night.'

Ellie's pulse quickened.

'You do?' she asked, neutrally.

'Don't you?' He seemed to pause slightly before replying. He seemed awfully tense.

'Of course I do,' she replied, softly. 'But whenever I've tried to be in touch with you, you... you didn't seem like you wanted to hear from me. And that morning, when I woke up, you'd gone. You didn't say goodbye.'

'Got called out for a rescue. Didn't want to wake you up.' He scuffed his foot in the sand. 'I wanted to say goodbye. But I didn't want you to go, either.'

'Oh.' Ellie looked down at the white sand under her feet. 'I missed you,' she murmured.

'Missed you too.' He took a deep breath, as if he had to prepare what he said next. 'Sorry I didn't text much. I never really know what to say.' He looked uncomfortable. 'I guess I wanted to see you in person.' He reached for her hand, and took it gently. Ellie took in a deep breath, remembering now the electricity that seemed to thrum between them. She had longed to feel this again all the time she was away.

'Well, here I am.'

'Yeah.'

Ellie waited for Mark to say something more, but he frowned

again and looked away. *If you've got something to say, then say it,* she thought, frustrated at his lack of eloquence. They were standing on the beach, on a sunny day, holding hands. If this wasn't a good time for Mark to make a move, then Ellie didn't know what was. She had told him she missed him. What more did he want?

'Ellie? I...' Mark took a deep breath. 'The thing is—'

'Ellie! There you are. I've been looking for you everywhere.' Rowland jogged towards them, holding two ice cream cones. His loud, eloquent voice carried across spaces well: he was used to projecting his voice in the courtroom, after all.

Instinctively, Ellie dropped Mark's hand as if she was doing something wrong by holding it.

'Oh, hi!' She shaded her eyes and smiled at Rowland, even thought she was annoyed at him for interrupting. It was a reflex: a social behaviour. Rowland had been her friend for a long time. She couldn't not say hello if he approached her.

But you made it look like nothing was happening with Mark, her mind whispered. *And it is. You'll have to tell Rowland at some point.*

'Sweets for the sweet.' Rowland handed her a vanilla cone. 'Sorry, I wasn't sure which one you'd want. The girl at the stall recommended the vanilla.'

'Oh. Thanks.' Ellie took it. Mark stood there like one of the slate boulders that lined the back of the cove: silent, sturdy and intractable. She wished he would say something easy and fun, to finesse the whole situation, but he stared silently at Rowland and crossed his arms over his chest.

'Rowland Hyatt. Nice to meet you.' Rowland held out the hand that didn't hold an ice cream, but Mark's arms stayed crossed.

'Mark Gardner,' he replied, giving the absolute minimal greeting possible.

'Mark repaired Marilyn, my motorhome,' Ellie explained.

'Oh, and he's Jamey Gardner's brother. You have her case coming up in family court, remember?'

'Oh, I *see*. Good, good. Well, you understand I can't talk about upcoming cases, of course. Lovely job on the motorhome, Gardner.' Rowland gave Ellie a bright smile. 'But I'm going to have to steal this one away for now. Important fundraiser business.' He took Ellie's hand and led her away, as if she was a stray dog. *'You're welcome,'* he murmured, evidently thinking that he was rescuing Ellie from an awkward social interaction. But Ellie saw that Mark had heard Rowland's not-so-quiet murmur, and she was annoyed. She knew that he could be the model of politeness when he wanted to be.

'I'll see you later?' Ellie called over her shoulder to Mark, but he had turned away and was walking up the beach. *I guess I'll never know what he was about to say*, she thought, annoyed at Rowland for whisking her away. Like he owned her.

'Rowland. Stop!' Ellie pulled her hand free from his. 'That was rude. I was talking to Mark and you came in and took over.'

'What? You looked bored.' Rowland spread out his hands in a 'sorry' gesture. 'The guy doesn't exactly seem that fascinating. These locals are all alike.'

'Well, I wasn't bored,' Ellie snapped. 'You don't own me. You don't have the right to decide who I get to talk to and when. And, actually, the locals here have been incredibly nice to me.'

'Oh, I see. We're playing the worthy game, I see.' Rowland rolled his eyes. 'Yes, yes, of course, all the locals are wonderful. Salt of the earth. Working-class gems. Like a Ken Loach film.'

'That's mean.'

'Come on. If you saw what I see through the family court every week you'd know what men like that are. Uneducated, ignorant, violent. You saw it for yourself – Darren Chivers almost killed you. You're too good for someone like that.' Rowland licked his ice-cream cone.

'We were just talking. My goodness, Rowland, I'm not marrying the man. And Mark is nothing like Darren Chivers.'

'Don't give me that. I saw the way he was looking at you. You were holding hands, for God's sake.'

Ellie took a step back, observing the change in Rowland from jolly and charming to icy cold and possessive. It wasn't a side of him she'd seen before, and she didn't like it at all.

'Rowland, what I do with Mark Gardner or anyone else is none of your business,' Ellie enunciated slowly. 'And I don't agree, about the people here. Wherever you worked, you'd see the bad side of people. You're a judge. It's like being a policeman. But you also get to see families reunited sometimes. Or children helped. Women protected. Not all people are bad, and it's nothing to do with class or location if they are or not.'

'Not like you have to get a first at Cambridge to fix cars.' Rowland sniffed.

'Okay. I'm going to walk away now before I lose even more respect for you.' Ellie shook her head. 'Rowland, I thought you were a good person.'

'I thought we had something.' Rowland reached for Ellie's wrist but she pulled away from him. 'I waited for you, Ellie. Look, you might like to think that you're able to leave the good life behind, but I know you. You're a bright, successful woman. You're used to a certain standard of living. You need someone like you. Your own kind.'

'My own kind is a human being who doesn't classify people according to how much money they earn. Anyway, Mark's not who you think he is,' she added, angrily. 'Please don't tell me what to do or who to like.'

'Hey. Rowland, right?' Fee, wearing a pink tankini, sauntered over. Ellie wondered if her friend radar had kicked in or whether she was just curious about meeting Rowland; Ellie had told her a few stories about him from the old days.

'Fee. Hi. I've heard so much about you. We were just talking.' He pushed his hair out of his eyes, sounding slightly self-conscious.

'Actually, we were just arguing,' Ellie gave Fee a fixed smile. 'And Rowland was just leaving.'

'Fine. I'm leaving. I'll call you, Ellie.' Rowland shrugged. 'When you've calmed down, you'll see I was right.'

'Don't call me!' Ellie yelled. 'I won't pick up.'

'Whatever. I'm not sure I was ever going to cope with the one breast thing anyway.' Rowland raised an eyebrow and turned away. 'Freakish'.

There was a silence: Ellie flinched at the word she had dreaded hearing.

'Jeez, man. That was low.' Fee hugged Ellie as Rowland walked off. 'You okay?'

'Yeah, I'm okay. Just found out who Rowland Hyatt really is, that's all.' She sighed.

'Aww, my cherub, are you all right?' Esther suddenly appeared next to her and enveloped Ellie in a hug. 'Did 'ee 'urt you, my love? D'you want to come and sit down? Come on. Talk to Esther.'

Ellie allowed herself to be guided to a nearby picnic bench under a beach umbrella. Clare had organised a couple of guys to come and lay them out on the beach earlier, and now they were full of picnicking families and other swimmers.

'I'm okay. Don't worry.' Ellie sat down on the wooden bench and gave Esther a weak smile. The word *freakish* hung in the air; it hurt to hear.

'Ah. Friend of yours, was he?' Esther regarded her with eyes that had probably seen every kind of argument and human frailty over the years.

'I thought he was.'

'Takes a long time to get to know who people really are. Past what they want to show you.' Esther stared out at the sea. 'I lost my 'usband a few years back now. We was together years. But there were still some days where I thought, *I dunno who this man is*. You can sleep in the same bed every night, you can 'ave children together. But one day they'll say somethin' or do somethin' that makes you think, *'Oo is this man*? 'Tis the way of things.'

'I suppose so.' Ellie frowned. 'Rowland thinks he knows me, but he doesn't, either.'

'There you are, then.' Esther clucked. 'I'd be jumpin' if anyone said that to me.'

'Jumping?' Ellie looked baffled.

'Jumpin' – angry.' Esther translated the Cornish phrase.

'Oh, right.' Ellie wondered if she'd ever get the hang of some of the old language that got mixed up with English down at the far end of the country.

Fee sat down next to Ellie. 'Aaagh. I'm boiling. Don't think we'll be seeing him again anytime soon.'

'Good,' Ellie tutted. 'He was being horrible. Even before you turned up. He was trying to persuade me that we were better than the people that come from Magpie Cove. Because we've got well-paid jobs and have been to university. But it was just snobbishness. I didn't think Rowland was like that.'

'Ellie, sorry to repeat this, but all of your London friends are dicks.' Fee laid a hand on Ellie's shoulder and looked her seriously in the eye. 'Except me, obviously.'

'No, they're not. They're just... different.' Ellie protested.

Fee shook her head. 'They're not bad people, but they live in a totally different world of privilege. You tried to keep up, but, ultimately, it's not who you are.'

'Toni's okay. We've been in touch,' Ellie protested. When she'd got back to London, she and Toni had had coffee a couple of times. It had been nice, and she knew Toni would always be there for her. But, at the same time, Ellie knew she'd changed.

'Who am I, then? I don't feel like I know anymore.' Ellie held her head in her hands. 'Esther, you must think I sound like such an idiot. I'm sorry for making you listen to all my personal crap like this.'

'Don't be silly, my love! I agree with Fee. You're a clever girl, just like my Connie, but she took a while to find 'er place in the world. I wanted 'er to settle down in Magpie Cove and get married 'an' 'ave kids, but she went off an' 'ad a career. I was cross about it, but then I realised she was right. She 'ad to be true to 'erself, and so do you. You don't 'ave ter 'ang on to the old things. Do what makes yer 'appy, that's my advice. Life's short.'

Ellie knew that as well as anyone. And, sitting on the beach at Magpie Cove, she realised what she had wanted all along. She shaded her eyes and looked back at Marilyn, glinting at the top of the beach.

'Fee, can you all cope without me for a bit? I've got to go and do something.'

'Going to see Mark?' Her friend shaded her eyes and gazed up at Ellie, who tried – and failed – to look outraged. 'Come on. You're as transparent as Marilyn's new headlights.'

'I might be,' Ellie tutted. 'It's none of your business.'

'Sure it is. But if you are going to find him, you might want to think about changing. That top's a bit sweaty.' Fee raised an eyebrow. 'Go and put a nice sundress on or something if you're going to make a romantic overture. And don't forget we've got the press coming along later. You have to do your interview.'

'I won't. Goodness.' Ellie felt like a child, being ordered around by a bossy teacher.

'Fine, then. Go and find your destiny.' Fee shooed her away. 'Go. You've got an hour. Make it count.'

TWENTY-NINE

Ellie had her T-shirt half off when someone knocked at Marilyn's door.

'Wait! Just a minute!' she yelled, tugging at it gently. At least she didn't have her drains in anymore, because they would have got pulled out straightaway, she thought. Hurriedly, she pulled on the pretty white linen sundress she'd brought down from London and adjusted her prosthetic breast. The dress buttoned up to the neck and had short sleeves, a full skirt and a wide white linen belt. *Good. Summery and demure, but nice,* she thought. It was a few sizes up from her old clothes, but she really didn't care.

She opened the door, and her heart fluttered. Ellie had imagined that she would have to go looking for Mark, but there he was, on her doorstep. If Fee had been there, she would have said something like, *The universe is making it as clear as humanly possible for you here, babes. You're a bright girl. Don't mess it up again.*

'Oh. Hello again.' Ellie ran a hand through her hair, wishing she'd had a chance to brush it.

'Hi.' Mark Gardner stood outside, holding a small bunch of roses wrapped in foil at the bottom. 'I brought you these. To say sorry about before.'

'Thank you.' Ellie took them. Now that she was with Mark, she didn't know what to say to him. She'd been thinking of all the things she wanted to say as she got changed: that she wanted to get to know him better. That she couldn't stop thinking about that one night they'd spent together. That his touch had been electric.

'From my garden,' he added. 'You'll want to put 'em in some water. Hot day like this.'

'Right. Come in. I'll find a glass or something.' Ellie opened Marilyn's kitchen cupboard where an array of plastic tumblers was lined up behind a metal bar to stop everything falling out.

'You've made some changes in here.' Mark looked around at the new curtains Ellie had had made, the updated carpet and new upholstery. 'This looks great.'

'Thanks.'

Ellie was nervous. She'd imagined running up to Mark, perhaps on top of the cliff overlooking Magpie Cove, her white dress billowing romantically in the wind. She'd imagined him catching her, and them both looking deep into each other's eyes and kissing, not saying anything. She hadn't quite imagined them slipping into a conversation about upholstery aboard her motorhome.

'Custom upholstery can be pricey.' Mark looked at his shoes.

'How did it turn out with Jamey? And how is she?' Ellie asked. 'I did try and keep in touch with Clare, but there's only so much she could tell me due to confidentiality, and it's not her case anyway. Plus, she hardly texts.'

'Good. I mean, *not* good. She's gonna take a long time to recover from what he did to her. What he did to you all. But he's got prison time. And he's not allowed to see the kids. All we could hope for, really. Jamey's gonna take the kids and move up to Exeter. He won't know where she's gone, and we've got family up there. New start. I'll still go up and see 'em, of course.'

'That's good.' Ellie breathed a sigh of relief. 'Poor Jamey. I was so scared that night. I can only imagine what it was like for her.'

'Yep.' He put his hands in his pockets.

'I'm not involved with Rowland,' she said, suddenly. 'I'm sorry about him, back there. We kissed, one night, that was all. He's an old friend.'

'More your type than I am,' Mark muttered. 'Lost my temper. I'm sorry. I just can't forget that night we spent together. It meant a lot to me.'

'It meant a lot to me too.' Ellie laid the flowers down in the motorhome's sink and stepped cautiously towards Mark. 'I didn't want you to think it didn't. And... I didn't just come back for the wild swim. I came back hoping to see you.'

'You sure? That guy's richer than me. I'm no good at conversation. You'd get bored with me.' Mark looked away from her.

Ellie stood closer to him; breathed in his subtle scent of honey and cotton.

'I can't get bored of this,' she murmured, as she kissed him. His lips tasted slightly of sea salt. She wrapped her arms around his neck. His hands found her waist and he returned her kiss, but then cleared his throat and broke away.

'Look. I got to explain something. Before this goes any further,' he said, running his hand through his rumpled hair. 'I'm not a man of many words. Right?'

'I noticed,' Ellie replied, steadily. 'But if you think I prefer Rowland to you, I really don't. Believe me.'

'I do. But listen. Okay?'

'Okay.' She sat down on the booth-style sofa that lined one wall of the motorhome. 'I'm listening.'

'Right. Thing is, since I was a kid, I've had a stammer. Used to get teased for it rotten. As I got older, I learned to control it. So I can speak properly, but I need to concentrate. That's why I don't talk much.'

'I had no idea.' Ellie leaned forward, wanting to touch him, wanting to make it all right. To show him that she didn't care about a stammer or anything else Mark might feel was slightly imperfect about himself.

'No, well. Most people don't. I've gone out with girls before and they got annoyed 'cos I don't talk much. Think I'm boring or something.'

'I don't think you're boring, Mark,' Ellie said in a low voice. 'I'm sorry about your stammer, but it really doesn't matter to me, I promise.'

'I know.' He beamed at her. 'Thing is, when it's just you and me, it's not hard to talk. I feel like I can chat away to you. I dunno why, but I do.'

'I've always felt that too. I've noticed that if other people are around, you're kind of quiet. I thought you were shy.'

'I'm not shy,' he murmured, taking her hand and leading her to the double bed in the back of the motorhome. 'Ellie. Stay with me. Stay with me. Here. In Magpie Cove. I want you to stay. Please.'

He laid her softly on the bed, kissing her. His fingers found the buttons on her dress and undid them slowly, one at a time. She whispered his name, reaching for him, wanting him.

Once more, Ellie felt self-conscious of her scar and her missing breast, but Mark kissed her chest and touched her so tenderly that she melted under his careful, loving hands. '*Trust me*,' he whispered. '*You know you can trust me*.' And she did.

Their bodies fitted perfectly together: everything about Mark Gardner was right and good and somehow *true*.

Afterwards, as they lay on top of the sheets, Ellie reached for Mark's hand and held it tight.

'What if I stayed?' she turned to him, propping herself on her elbow.

'In Magpie Cove? I'd be happy if you did.' Mark sat up in bed. 'But... you've got your job in London. What would you do here?'

'I could sell my flat, or rent it out.' Ellie watched his face for signs he was lying; that, like Rowland, he only wanted one part of her. But Mark's expression was full of hope. 'I've been in touch with a women's charity that needs some legal expertise. I can work remotely for most of the time. Travel for some meetings.' She paused. 'There's one problem, though.' Ellie made herself look serious.

'What?'

'I'd need somewhere for Marilyn. Like, maybe a local mechanic who has a large garage space. Can you think of anyone who fits that description?' She grinned, tickling Mark's ribs.

'Hmmm. Maybe. I'll ask around.' He grabbed her hand and held it, tickling her instead.

'Mark! Stop it. I've got to go and meet this journalist for the local paper in a minute.' Ellie giggled, fending off the tickle attack.

'Sleeping with a celebrity, am I?' he asked, holding her close to him and kissing her forehead. 'Blimey. Lucky me.'

'You're bloody lucky, let me tell you.' Ellie kissed him, full on the lips, and then sighed. 'Okay. I really have to get up now.'

She sat up and reached for her dress, buttoning it carefully.

'You're really going to stay?' Mark watched her. 'Where will you live?

'Maybe. Yes. I'll find somewhere.' Ellie gazed out of the window at the beach house. 'You know, I think Mara's going to put the beach house up for sale soon. When it's been repaired and renovated.'

'Good investment for someone selling a flat in London...'

Mark commented, following her gaze. 'And that person could stay with a local mechanic in the meantime if she wanted.'

'I think she would like that.' Ellie smiled, reaching for a brush and tidying her hair. 'There. Do I look presentable?'

'You're perfect.' Mark gazed at her. 'Never known anyone look as perfect as you, Ellie McTavish.'

THIRTY

'And I'm delighted to announce that we've raised... wait for it...' Clare adjusted her glasses on her nose and peered at a piece of paper Mara handed to her '£5,235! That's an amazing achievement, I'm sure you'll agree. Thank you all for coming to the inaugural Magpie Cove Wild Swim. It's been our first, but we hope it won't be the last!'

A cheer went up from the crowd. Ellie and Mark stood at the back; he reached for her hand. How long had it been since she had felt this connection with a man? Had she ever? She didn't think she had. There had been men, but she had never really trusted any of them with her heart. But now, when she was at her most vulnerable, she had allowed Mark in. And he had shared his vulnerability with her too.

'Ellie! Where did you get to? Oh, never mind.' Petra ran up to them from one of the stalls. 'I see. Hi, Mark.' She grinned at Ellie. 'The reporter's here from the newspaper. Can you do it now?'

'Sure. I'll come and find you later, okay?' She detached her hand from Mark's.

'Make sure you do.' He smiled, giving her a shy look from under his eyelashes.

Clare passed Ellie as she headed off the stage. 'Oh, Ellie. I'm glad I've caught you.' She tapped Ellie on the arm.

'I've just got to do this newspaper interview, Clare – I'll be back soon, though,' Ellie said. She felt unreasonably nervous. It was only a local rag, but somehow, the thought of telling her story was still scary. Anyone might read it, and judge her somehow.

'No probs. I wanted to let you know that there's some part-time work that's come up at my firm, if you were interested. Not as highbrow as you're used to, but we'd love to have you. Or even some consulting might work.'

'Wow. Okay, thanks. I'll think about it.' Ellie gazed at the beach house. Could she live in Magpie Cove? It seemed like the stars were aligning to make her stay.

'Do! Say yes. We need someone like you here,' Clare added. 'Now, go on and be wonderful!'

'Clare, please say a big thanks to whoever your colleague was who helped with Jamey's case. It really means a lot.' Ellie enveloped Clare in a sudden heartfelt hug. 'And thank you for everything you did too.'

'Oh, you're welcome, silly! Just doing my job,' Clare said, looking pleased. 'Now. Go on!'

Ellie was relieved to see that the local journalist was a woman. She was sitting at one of the picnic tables looking at her phone. Ellie took a deep breath.

You can do this. It's okay, she told herself. Every time she talked about her cancer, it got easier. And if it helped someone else to read about her journey, then her nerves would be worth it. She thought about how scared she'd been, going into surgery. How she had asked the universe to get her through it, alive. And it had. It had brought her to Magpie Cove, and as soon as she'd stepped foot in the village, her life had changed forever.

She thought again about that doctor telling her about *survival rates*; about him saying, *Don't worry, we'll make you look normal again.* She'd been considering breast reconstruction surgery, and she hadn't come to a decision yet.

But, maybe, she was normal exactly the way she was. She didn't have to have that surgery if she didn't want to. Mark certainly didn't seem to mind her scar.

Feel the fear and do it anyway, she told herself. Wasn't that what people said? She had already done so much that she was afraid of. She could do a newspaper interview. In fact, it was the least scary thing she'd done in months.

'Hi, I'm Ellie.' She approached the woman and held out her hand.

'Hi, Ellie. I'm Romola. Ready to talk? I just have a few questions, then I'll be out of your hair.' The woman smiled warmly.

'I'm ready.' Ellie breathed in the fresh sea air and sent a little prayer of thanks up to the sun that warmed her skin. 'Let's do it.'

LONDON WOMAN FINDS NEW LIFE IN MAGPIE COVE

A high-flying London lawyer has inspired the people of Magpie Cove to fundraise for a cancer charity

by Romola Rose

Ellie McTavish, a thirty-seven-year-old woman from London, has led a recent fundraising campaign to help women in Magpie Cove access cervical and breast screening services.

McTavish, a corporate lawyer, arrived in Magpie Cove by accident a few months ago when her vintage motorhome broke down just outside the village. Having to stay in the village until the vehicle could get repaired, McTavish – who had recently been treated for breast cancer – became friends with a group of wild swimmers in the village and proposed the inaugural Magpie Cove Wild Swim event as a cancer fundraiser. The wild swim has raised over £5,000 for local cancer charities, and the group plans to fund a private bus service running from Magpie Cove to Truro, the closest clinic that can provide mammograms, breast checks, cervical screening and other vital healthcare. The Magpie Cove Wild Swim is planned to be an annual event.

Speaking to this interviewer, Ellie McTavish said: 'I was lucky that I had a doctor who acted quickly on my behalf when I found a lump in my breast. This meant that I got surgery within two weeks, and now have a good chance that I can remain cancer free because of my doctor's speedy diagnosis.

'When I heard that the women of Magpie Cove were being denied essential cancer screening because of budget cuts, my friends and I in the wild swimming group felt that we had to do something, so the Magpie Cove Wild Swim was conceived. We really hope that it will help draw the council's attention to restoring a very necessary service for women in remote coastal areas, as well as boosting awareness of the importance of getting regular breast and cervical screening. Wild swimming is a healing and transformative activity, and swimming generally is a brilliant exercise particularly for women recovering from a mastectomy or breast surgery. If you get a chance to do it, take it – you won't regret it.'

When I asked her what she thought of Magpie Cove itself, Ms McTavish paused for a few moments and then told me: 'I can honestly say that my motorhome breaking down outside Magpie Cove was the best thing that ever happened to me. When I was a little girl, I used to dream about coming on holiday to the seaside. It seemed like a place of freedom and adventure, but my mum could never really afford to take us on holiday. Then, when I was an adult and I could afford it, I went abroad, often to five-star resorts and luxury yachts. But I was never really that happy. I left Magpie Cove to go back to London six weeks ago, and I've hated every minute being away from this little village. Partly, I missed my friends, and going swimming every day, and seeing the sun rise over the sea. The glow of the moon on the water at night, and the magpies cackling as they fly over the houses.

'But, if I'm honest, there's also a special someone that I missed most of all. And I want to take this opportunity to tell him – and tell everyone – what an amazing man he is. Mark Gardner has a gift. It's not the gift of the gab, like some, but talk is cheap when it's not followed by actions. Mark's gift is bringing the best out of everything and everyone, whether that's turning my clunky old motorhome into a vintage treasure, making delicious meals out of simple ingredients or making buns out of flour, yeast and seeds. But it's more than that, too. He helped me regain my confidence – in my body, and in myself – at a time when I thought I would never feel like a successful woman again. Mark Gardner helped me believe in myself.

'Once, I thought that my work made me successful. Or the money that I'd earned in my job, and the luxurious lifestyle it bought me. But that wasn't right.

'I'm successful because I beat cancer, and I was brave enough to let someone like Mark come into my life and not push him away out of fear. And I'm brave enough to leave my old life in London behind and start again here, if Magpie Cove – and Mark – will have me.'

The *Cornish Star* wishes Ellie McTavish all the very best of luck with her new life in Cornwall.

A LETTER FROM KENNEDY

Hi! I hope you enjoyed *Dreams of Magpie Cove*. If you did enjoy it and want to keep up to date with all my latest releases, just sign up at the following link. Your email address will never be shared and you can unsubscribe at any time.

www.bookouture.com/kennedy-kerr

Ellie's story in this book was inspired by my own mother's experience with breast cancer, and the knowledge that so many women experience this distressing and difficult illness. Like Ellie, my mum had radiation therapy and then took a drug, Tamoxifen, after having a mastectomy, and the treatments combined were very effective. I vividly remember the surgical drain that Mum came home from the hospital with, and so made sure that I mentioned that in Ellie's story too. I wanted Ellie's story ultimately to be positive, but not to deny the fact that breast cancer is a big deal and takes a lot to recover from. I hope I've done that.

I researched the best exercise after a mastectomy and it turned out that swimming is a really good thing to do as it can help feeling return to the chest and underarm area, but is a gentle exercise. Wild swimming had actually been suggested to me by my editor Kelsie Marsden as a possible activity that might work well in Magpie Cove, and the two themes seemed to mesh well together. Additionally, I have always thought of Magpie Cove as a place people go to heal, usually emotionally, but it was good to add in the healing power of the salt water of the cove here too. I have always felt there was something healing about beaches: the salt water, the fresh air and the sand underfoot.

Like the other subjects I have covered in the Magpie Cove series, breast cancer (and domestic violence, as experienced by Jamey) is something that women can feel reluctant to talk about. I hope that Ellie's and Jamey's experiences can act as an encouragement to talk to others, should this be happening to you or someone you know. As ever, talking is important, and being heard and loved is the most important thing of all.

With all my good thoughts,

Kennedy

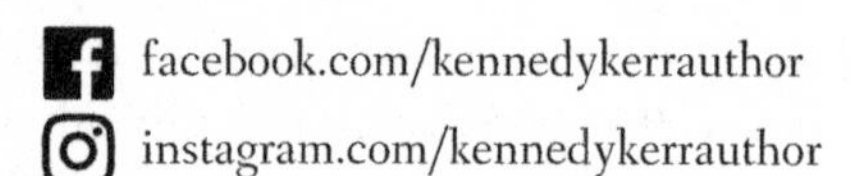

ACKNOWLEDGEMENTS

Thank you to Kelsie Marsden who suggested the theme of wild swimming to me at the Bookouture summer party: it was a great idea! I hope you don't mind me using it. Thank you also to my wonderful editor and publisher Kathryn, who has helped mould and refine the Magpie Cove books so well, and who has an inimitable instinct for what works – and doesn't work! – in a book like this.

Fans of Melissa McCarthy movies may notice that I used an homage to Kristen Wiig's line about the character Kevin (played by Chris Hemsworth) from her *Ghostbusters* remake: *'Pure muscle. Oh, and baby-soft skin'* when Fee hugs Mark at the end of the book. If I could choose anyone to play Mark in a film version of this book, it would be Chris Hemsworth, or a 1990s-era Brad Pitt. Also, I am a huge fan of Melissa McCarthy and her empowering yet hilarious movies, so thank you to Melissa too.

Made in the USA
Coppell, TX
26 April 2023